I0549220

Am I
Dreaming?

Am I Dreaming?

Justin Weiher

Am I Dreaming?
Justin Weiher

Published by Justin Weiher, Edmonton, Canada

ISBN   978-1-77354-256-0   paperback

         978-1-77354-260-7   electronic book

Dedication

A portion of proceeds from this book will be donated to organizations that support victims of domestic violence/abuse.

1

The Chase (Get Out!)

can feel my heart beating out of my chest, but I know I can't slow down or he'll catch me. I have shooting pain in my feet from running and stepping on broken glass as I climbed out the window. Why is this happening to me? What did I do to deserve this?

As I continue running, I feel the rain start to fall as each drop hits my head and eyes, making it even more difficult to see where I am going. It doesn't help that it is around five o'clock in the morning and almost everything is closed. I hear the thunder cracking and the rain slamming against the ground, getting louder and louder. I am briefly lost as I have been running for about 10 minutes now – who knows as time feels like it is standing still.

I stop for a moment to take a look at my surroundings: suddenly a loud clap of thunder makes me jump and I begin running yet again. This has got to be a nightmare. Surely I'll wake up soon and this will all be over.

At this point there's no turning back, I need to get out of here, I need Jess. As I continue running I feel something stinging on my thigh. I hadn't notice it before, but I look down and see the rain washing blood down my leg. I likely had too much adrenaline to feel any pain at the time it happened. Maybe I caught myself on the edge of the broken window when I climbed out. It is starting to hurt like hell but I have to stay focused and find my way out of here. Through the trees I can see some lights: maybe they are from the train station in town. "Why did I move outside of town?" I think to myself. Nobody around to help me! I don't want to die.

Tears begin running down my face as the fear and realization of the situation flood over me. I head towards the lights, hoping there is someone there who can help me. The lights are getting closer, then another loud crackling sound from the sky, freezing me in the moment. I fall towards the ground, my body slamming down into the muddy, wet leaves. My body aches everywhere, I'm covered in mud, and my leg is still bleeding. I look up and see the light at the building go out. That must mean someone is there; if I don't get up now and make it there, this could be my last chance. There is no stopping him: he will find me and this time there's no telling what he will do. I lean against a tree beside me to help pull my body up and I head for what seems like the only place I can go for help.

As I get closer I can finally see someone leaving the building. I scream for help but as I do, the thunder and rain drown out my voice. They continue walking towards their car. I scream again but they don't hear me. I am not as fast as I could be as I have been running for what feels like forever, have a big cut on my leg, and no shoes. As I see the end of the tree line and approach the building, all I can see is the back of the car as it drives away. It is the train station though, but I don't know if another train is coming as I have never taken one and it is the middle of the night.

If another train doesn't come, I am screwed. There is nothing else around. It's only about 100 yards away and then I see a train coming. I have to make it there before it leaves. As I limp my way to the station, I hear a whistle, which I can only assume means that it's ready to depart. I see the fence to access the train and scurry to reach the door. I frantically push the button repeatedly to open the doors. They finally do and I roll my soaking body into the train car. The doors shut and the train starts moving.

I can't believe I made it and I don't see him anywhere. Maybe I got lucky this time.

2

How It All Started

could not be more excited to start my freshman year in college next week. For as long as I can remember I have wanted to work with criminals and why they do the things they do. I decided to apply for my psych degree, in hopes of one day getting my doctorate. My dad is a forensic psychologist and now I am finally following in his footsteps.

He never pushed me in the direction of his career path, but naturally hearing all of his stories at the dinner table, I had a curiosity about the field that I could not deny. When I told him I wanted to go into this program he was very supportive and proud, although he did caution me that this area of work does take a toll on a person.

I remember he would always say "You can't take your work home with you or you will go crazy", but I could see at times that he was bothered by the stuff he dealt with. Even though a person tries to be professional and is trained to do so, being exposed to situations and circumstances like he was daily would have an effect on someone. I vowed to not let the work affect me, but my dad just smiled and said he thought the same thing when he started.

I had a great summer hanging out with friends and being single, as I had just broken up with my high school sweetheart shortly after grad. It's not that I didn't love Jordan anymore, I just think we were heading in different directions in life and because I was going to a college across the country, the long distance thing would just be too difficult. We told each other we would remain close friends and keep in contact no matter what, and if our lives brought us back together somehow, then it was meant to be.

My friends and I spent most of our time at the lake that summer before I headed out for school as we knew we likely wouldn't be spending as much time together in the future. Occasionally I would see Jordan there too and make conversation. One night there was a big party and we ended up making out again. We never really did anything more than kissing except for that one time when I let him go down on me, but that was it. I was saving myself for marriage or at least for the guy I planned to spend my life with.

I know kissing Jordan again was a big mistake as it brought back all those feelings and even made him think I wanted to try our relationship again. I felt bad telling him I didn't and that it was just the moment and all those feelings of familiarity and history. He seemed to understand, but I could tell that he still wanted to be with me. For the next couple of weeks I didn't talk to him and figured I better lay low because I didn't want to hurt him more.

With a week before school starting I planned on arriving there a few days early to get my dorm room set up and familiarize myself with the campus. Before I left, however, I had to buy a few things for the first semester. Dad took me shopping which I thought was cute. He bought me supplies, clothes, and even some things for my new dorm room. I was eighteen and could have bought for myself, but he still wanted to go with me and be part of the experience. I guess he knew it was going to be his last time doing this before I left the nest so I let him have his moment, plus I enjoyed his company. I was going to miss him a lot as we had a special relationship and I had never been away from home, but I was excited about this new chapter in my life and felt like I was about to start something worthwhile.

Admittedly I was a little nervous as I did not know what to expect: would I pass my courses, would I know where I am going, how would I adjust to being away from home on my own, would I meet a nice guy to take my mind off Jordan? So many questions racing through my head all week leading up to me going to orientation at the college.

Saturday morning finally came and I jumped out of bed excited to get going to my new life, my new home, at least for the next four years. The drive seemed long, even though it was only about an hour and a half, but you know when you are looking forward to something, how it seems to take forever to get to that place. I am glad my dad came with me though as we were able to spend some quality time together talking about memories, and as my dad consistently does, brag about how proud he was of me and also how careful I needed to be now that I would be living on my own on a college campus.

He's always been the type to worry too much, but I guess that's what parents do, and that's part of what makes him such a great dad is that he cares so much.

When we arrived there were so many people walking everywhere. I had no idea where to go, but thankfully a girl who looked like she was part of the campus, as she was wearing a college shirt and some sort of button that said "Welcome new students", asked me if I needed some help. I told her I was new to campus and needed to register and find my dorm. She was very energetic and told me all about the activities for the first week and where the main hubs were, then pointed me towards the administration building to get enrolled and find my dorm.

I wanted to go check in myself, but of course my dad insisted he help bring my things to my room and see it for himself. I figured I wouldn't argue with him and let him have this one, since he would be seeing less of me in the future, and also probably wanted to check out that I don't have some weirdo for a roommate who he would have to worry about as well.

My dorm building was all-female which I know made my dad happy, and I guess it was cool with me too. Hopefully I could make some new friends without having a distraction of boys. Thankfully the administration office said they allowed parents to go inside to help in the first week of moving in, but other than that, boys were not permitted. My dad reminded me on the drive to the college that he was paying a lot of money for my education and that I had to keep my grades up if I wanted to get into grad school, so basically don't let boys get in the way.

As I approached my room there was a smell that caught my attention, kind of like an orangey scent, but I couldn't quite tell what it was or where exactly it was coming from. At least it didn't smell bad because I hate when you go into a building and the first thing you notice is a bad smell. I'm not sure I could handle that for the next four years so I'll take the unknown orange smell.

I knocked on my door and nobody answered, so I turned the knob and opened the door slowly to the unexpected. There was nobody else in the room and there was a decent amount of space for two people. The walls were pretty bare but one side had a picture on it of some sort of abstract art. The future psychologist in me was drawn to this picture so I decided to set my things down on that side of the room. I hoped my new roommate wouldn't mind that I picked it, but I thought it was fair from a first-come first-served perspective.

My dad gave his usual critique of things, saying how it was kind of dark in there and not much room to study, but I told him I would be fine and not to worry. He then proceeded to ask if I needed any money and reminded me that he was just a phone call away if anything ever happened, that he could be here in less than the time it took to drive here this morning. I told him I would be fine and also thanked him for everything he had done for me.

I gave him a big hug and kiss and told him I would see him next weekend when I came back home to visit. I could see he was getting a little emotional as a little tear came trickling out of his right eye. He told me how much he loved me and then said he was going to go and let me get settled in.

As I watched him walk down the hall I had mixed emotions. On the one hand I was sad to see him go as I have not been away from my mom or dad my entire life and I would obviously miss them, but on the other hand I was gaining independence and finally felt like I was starting my life. As he got to the end of the hall, he turned and looked at me one last time, gave a smile and a wave, to which I smiled back and returned the gesture. He turned the corner and was gone.

About thirty minutes after my dad left and I was almost done unpacking most of my things, I heard a knock at the door and said "come in", to which the door slowly opened and a blonde girl wearing jeans and a hoodie entered. She introduced herself as Jessica and seemed very nice. She was pretty and even kind of dressed like me so I thought that was a good start.

Her dad was also with her, which I thought was funny because we already had overprotective parents in common. He introduced himself as well and seemed like a good guy. He even cracked a joke which made me laugh, but then I could tell he was having a tough time leaving his daughter as well. They eventually said their goodbyes and then it was just the two of us.

We began chatting about where each of us were from and some of our interests; we also found out that we were in the same degree program and compared classes, many of which we would be taking together. This was going so well. I had met a great girl who seemed to have similar interests and since we were taking the same courses, we could study together and not feel so alone in this new adventure.

After getting settled in, we decided to walk around and familiarize ourselves with the campus and amenities. I could not believe how big the place was, especially compared to the small town I grew up in. There was a huge pool with steam rooms and separate sauna, a gym with every piece of exercise equipment you could imagine, several cafeterias, and little shops to buy things like incidentals and even clothes.

One of the things Jessica and I both noticed was the variety of people we continued to walk by: there were so many different cultures and ages of people too. I don't want to sound like I am judging people because that is not how I was raised, but by first impressions, there were a lot of "different" individuals.

Where I am from, even having two earrings in your ear gets you looks, but here people had nose rings, tongue rings, crazy haircuts and even their clothes were odd. This wasn't the norm, but we definitely came across quite a few of these interesting individuals in the hour we walked around campus. I should add that we did notice a lot of cute guys in our travels, but my dad's voice kept replaying in my head, "focus on school and don't let boys get in the way". So I just smiled in passing and didn't talk to any boys….for now.

After walking around most of the campus and finding everything, we ended up at the bookstore. We needed to get our books as classes started in two days and we wanted to make sure we had everything and started off on the right foot. Plus, we found a flyer by one of the cafeterias that said there was some sort of orientation for new students and that everyone should come participate as a good way to meet people. It also said there would be a free breakfast and when you are a student, anything free is a bonus.

Jessica and I collected all the books we needed and headed back to our dorm room. It was so nice that my dad had bought me a prepaid college card with a balance that could be used for anything on campus; food, drinks, books, clothing, etc. and each month he said he would reload it. This way I wouldn't have to worry about needing money, but if I wanted extra spending money I would have to get a part-time job. I didn't really want to get a job while in school, and I know my dad preferred if I didn't, but I guess I would see how it went.

When we were walking around we grabbed a coffee at the coffee shop on campus called "Books & Beans", and they had a sign saying "Help Wanted". I'm not in a rush to work, but it's good to know they are looking for more staff so I'll keep it in mind. Extra money is never a bad thing, especially for a girl who likes to shop.

That night Jessica and I stayed in our room and just chatted for hours, getting to know each other better and found out that we were more alike than we thought. Our birthdays were only two days apart, we each had a younger brother, and we were both were in gymnastics when we were younger. I had a few good friends in high school, but nobody that I considered my best friend or with whom I would share anything. As far as I could see, Jessica fit the bill in being that kind of friend.

It was getting pretty late and as we had that orientation in the morning, we decided to get some sleep.

The next morning we went to the communal showers to get ready, but I have never had to share a large bathroom with so many girls before so it was definitely an adjustment for me. I guess I had to get used to it as this would be my life for the next four years. There had to be at least ten girls in the bathroom that morning when Jessica and I went, and with only eight showers and six sinks, you can imagine the gossip that began as others waited to use the next free sink or shower. It wasn't too bad though because it was the beginning of the school year and most girls were new and didn't know anyone so everyone seemed to be friendly.

While I was brushing my teeth a couple girls came in and you could tell that this wasn't their freshman year and they even had a bit of snobby attitude as if they thought their crap didn't stink. I didn't really think much of it, but I did notice how one girl who was about to use one of the showers abruptly offered it to the brunette who had just walked in. I wondered what her deal was and why others felt they had to give in to her. I heard her friend call her "Brittany" so I made sure to keep that name in mind as it might come in handy later. She came up to the sink next to me and kind of gave me a look and then said, "Nice lipstick". I wasn't sure if she was being sarcastic or nice, so I simply said "thanks" and she didn't reply.

As I continued to do my makeup to get ready for the day, I could hear Brittany and her friend talking about some guy who she hooked up with and then her saying how she didn't care that he had a girlfriend and just needed a good fling now and then.

I hated girls like her: girls who think they can seduce another guy even when they know they have a girlfriend, just because they think it makes them so special that some guy will drop his pants for her even if he's in a relationship. She thinks she's all that because guys throw themselves at her, but in reality she's obviously insecure about something and using her looks and sexuality to make up for it.

I'm glad I heard all their gossip and know to stay away from that one as she is basically drama that I don't need.

We tried to hurry and finish getting ready so we could get to the breakfast in the common area and see what the orientation had to offer. While standing in line waiting to get food Jessica and I chatted and debated whether our line or the other line on the other side of the buffet row would be quicker. It turns out our line was moving faster so we stayed put. I could smell the bacon and was getting hungrier by the minute. As I finally reached the trays of food, I stuck the spoon in to scoop some eggs, another spoon bumped into mine. "Sorry," I heard, and I looked up and there was this very attractive guy smiling at me who had been trying to scoop eggs at the same time.

"No worries," I softly replied, with a smile of my own. He suggested I go ahead and continue scooping, to which I said "thank you".

He introduced himself, "I'm Tom, what's your name?" I broke eye contact and looked down at the bacon in the next bin of food.

"Kerry" I replied. I tried not to smile, but I was kind of nervous as he was quite good looking.

He asked me if it was my first year at college and I nodded. "What about you?" I asked.

"Yeah, first year, exciting isn't it?" he responded.

"Yeah, looking forward to it" I said with some enthusiasm, but didn't want to come across as too eager.

As we approached the end of the food line, he leaned somewhat toward me and with a smile said, "I'll see you around...Kerry", to which I smiled and turned the other direction. Jessica was right behind me and began smiling and asking me what that was all about. I said nothing, but she said "I saw how he looked at you". "You should have asked for his number" she added.

I told her I don't want to get involved with anyone right now and just need to focus on school. She said "I get that, but he was hot".

The orientation began by someone announcing the start of the school year and wishing everyone a safe and productive semester. They proceeded to explain the variety of activities they had planned for everyone to enjoy and get to know one another. Jessica and I decided to play some volleyball as we are both athletic and it looked like fun. After about thirty minutes of playing, I noticed Tom had joined the game on the other side. We exchanged a few smiles but didn't talk to each other. Jessica and I left about fifteen minutes later and Tom stayed back to continue playing. As I walked away however, I could feel his eyes on me and asked Jessica if he was looking. She confirmed with a "oh yeah, he's got eyes on you girl". I smiled as we walked away. Remember what dad said, I kept telling myself.

Jessica and I walked around the campus a bit more, looking for the buildings where most of our classes would be and stopping for another free bite as they had a free BBQ for everyone with hotdogs and hamburgers. They even had a beer garden area with loud music playing. Jessica and I walked by it as we ate our lunch, but it looked quite busy so we decided to pass on it. As we came back to our dorm there was a table outside with a couple girls sitting at it asking girls to join their sorority. Jessica and I looked at one another to see if each other was interested.

"You want to?" Jessica asked.

"I guess. What do we have to do?" I asked the girls at the table.

"Just a little initiation and then you're in," one of the girls replied.

"Okay" I replied. I've always heard about sororities and thought maybe it would be fun to be part of one. We signed up and gave our room number, then were told they would let us know when the initiation would occur. We went inside to our room to relax for a bit as we'd had a pretty busy day.

Later that evening we decided to go to one of the local pubs they had on campus for a bite to eat, but didn't want to make a late night of it as we started classes the next morning. The pub was called 'Pool Shark' as they had pool tables and some sort of ocean theme with seafood, burgers, and other food items. We sat at a table near the corner of the pub where it was a little quieter as the music was kind of loud. We each ordered a Bellini to celebrate the start of the school year and a seafood platter to share; the food was amazing!

About forty minutes later as we were almost done with our food and drinks, I couldn't help but notice someone sitting at the bar....it was Tom. I know there were only a few places to eat on campus, but I started to wonder if it was a coincidence that I saw him at the volleyball game and now again at the bar the same day. Maybe I was over-thinking it; I mean we both lived on campus so the odds of running into one another were going to be pretty high.

As Jessica and I walked towards the doors to head back to our dorm, Tom noticed me, reached out and touched my arm and said "Kerry, right?" as if to make note that he remembered me, but not entirely certain of my name. I replied, "Yeah", gave a smile, and then said "goodnight", to which he replied with a smile and reciprocated with "night".

As Jessica and I walked back to our dorm, I felt that same feeling of uncertainty whether it was coincidence or not and had to ask Jessica's opinion. She laughed and said I was reading into it too much. I responded by saying "I guess you're right" and we continued to our room. Tired by the busy day and thoughts of starting my post-secondary career tomorrow, I lay in bed trying to fall asleep, but also could not help but think about my several encounters with Tom today. On one hand I was intrigued as he was very attractive, but seeing him three times in one day was a little strange. I ended up concluding that it was likely just a coincidence and I drifted off to sleep.

3

First Day of Class

woke up feeling excited about the first day of classes and going to the orientation the previous day helped reduce some of my anxiety. I went to the showers early so I wouldn't have to wait for a free shower. As I stood there with the hot water running down my back, I couldn't help but wonder if I would see Tom today, but my thoughts were interrupted by the voices of girls coming into the washroom. One voice sounded familiar: I think it was that Brittany girl. I couldn't make out everything she was saying but I did hear her talking about some other girls and basically trash-talking them.

This girl sure thinks she's all that and acts like she runs this place. I also heard her mention that she couldn't wait to see the new sorority girls and initiate them, to which the girls with her all laughed. "Are you kidding me, she's one of the girls doing the initiation?" I thought to myself. As I stopped my shower, their voices seemed to lower immediately. After getting dressed I came out to do my makeup and Brittany and her friends were still there.

She looked me up and down as if to measure me up and judge me based on my clothes. She smiled, but it seemed fake. Then they all walked out together. For some reason she just makes me feel uncomfortable, but I didn't do anything to her so I wasn't sure what her deal was. Maybe she just acts that way to intimidate others and feel superior.

As I walked across campus towards my first class there were so many students going in every direction, all scurrying to start their semester on time. I remembered this building from my walk with Jessica the previous day and was happy I hadn't gotten lost on my first day. As I walked into the lecture room I couldn't believe how big it was: where I came from, the biggest class size had about 30 people in it. This room must have had 200 seats or more and was about half full already. I figured I would sit somewhere in the middle so I could see the professor well enough, but also blend in so I wouldn't be picked out of the crowd to answer any questions.

As students continued to move into their seats, I kept looking around to see if I knew anyone, specifically whether Tom was in this class. There was no sign of him, yet. I looked at the clock. Class was about to begin and so I took a deep breath and thought to myself, "here we go". The professor began speaking, introducing himself as Professor David Bennett and going over the course outline and expectations for the semester. The class was practically full with a few empty seats and everyone's eyes were glued to the professor. He was a good-looking man and probably in his late thirties, maybe forty, so not that old for a professor. I couldn't see a wedding ring on his finger from where I was sitting so I wasn't sure whether or not he was married or had a family. Not sure why I thought of these things when I should be listening to what he was saying, but sometimes the mind drifts to random thoughts.

Every so often I would glance around to look at some of the other students: some were typing on their laptops, some were likely catching up on Facebook posts, and others were taking notes by hand. As I listened to the professor lecture and making my own notes, I heard a faint noise, what sounded like a door close, but I didn't really pay any attention to it. A few minutes later as Professor Bennett took a brief break to grab a drink of water, I took another glance around over my shoulder and two rows back and about five seats over I saw Tom. It must have been him arriving late when I had heard the door close a few minutes earlier. He looked over at me as I turned and our eyes met for a moment. I smiled, he smiled back and I turned my attention back to the front of the class. Initially I felt a little giddy that he was in my class and I would obviously be seeing much more of him throughout the semester. For a brief moment however, I wondered why he was in my class and whether this was just another coincidence.

As the bell rang, I gathered my things and then I could feel someone coming near me. "Hey Kerry." My stomach instantly had knots but I replied "Hey". "How did you like the first class?" he asked.

"It was interesting," I replied.

As I started heading out of the lecture hall he walked with me. I didn't mind, but admittedly I was a little nervous. "I was wondering if you would like to grab a coffee sometime," he asked. At this point I was very intrigued by him, even though a part of me knew I shouldn't get involved, but I responded by saying "Sure, that would be great". We exchanged phone numbers and decided that the next day would work as I had a free block in the afternoon. We agreed to meet at Books & Beans. He extended his hand like a gentleman to seal the deal and told me to have a good day and that he was looking forward to having coffee with me and getting to know me. I smiled and could feel myself biting my bottom lip. Our handshake lasted longer than a normal handshake and there was definitely some sort of chemistry happening. As I walked away, I could almost feel him watching me, but I didn't turn around as I wanted to play it cool and not show I was too excited.

I met up with Jessica in my next class as we shared Introductory Psychology 101 together. She could tell I was glowing and immediately asked why I was so happy. I asked if she remembered the guy we had seen at the orientation and the Pool Shark the previous night and she nodded. I told her that he was in my first class and had come up to talk to me after class and ask me out for coffee. Her jaw opened and then she smiled and asked what I had said to him.

After telling her I agreed to meet him she said with a smile "Good for you, but just make sure you be careful, there's a lot of weirdos out there." I asked why she said that as if I wondered whether she had any reservations about him, even though she didn't really know him.

"Don't you think it's a little odd that he showed up at three places we were, in the same day? Maybe it's just a coincidence. Go enjoy a coffee and see what he's like. It's not like you're going to marry him," she chuckled.

After class Jessica and I went to grab some lunch together and we chatted about our first few classes and how, although exciting to be learning all these new things, we had pretty heavy workloads. About halfway through lunch, my phone dinged. It was a text. As I reached in my purse to grab my phone I wondered whether it was my dad checking up on me. My phone read "Message from Tom". Again I had butterflies in my stomach. I opened the message; "Hey Kerry, just wanted to see if you gave me a real number, lol. I'm looking forward to coffee tomorrow." I smiled and showed Jessica. "He's into you, girl" she replied. I replied back with a smiley face and said "me too". We both had the same class together after lunch and figured we had better leave soon so we could grab good seats and not be stuck at the front of the class.

That night I stayed in my dorm room and worked on homework. I didn't have a lot as it was only the first day, but I wanted to make sure I started off the year right and didn't fall behind. This was my future and I had to stay on top of my studies as I had a long road ahead of me. While I was reading my text, my thoughts drifted now and then to thinking about Tom and meeting him the next day, and then thoughts of my dad telling me to focus on school and not boys, but there was something very intriguing about Tom that I couldn't ignore. I guess I would see how tomorrow went and go from there.

After finishing my notes, I thought I would read a little ahead in my text, but felt my eyes starting to drift as it was getting pretty late. Just before I fell asleep my eyes caught that picture on the wall again. I had tried several times to find the meaning behind it but it still just looked like a bunch of colors blended together.

The next morning I was eager to get to class and see what we would be learning as I had registered for a human sexuality course. Every course was new for me, but this one I was particularly interested in. Being a virgin didn't mean I didn't have desires and was not interested in sex. I just want to save myself for the right person: I am a very passionate and affectionate person. As the class began, the professor went over the course outline and then shared a video with the class. This video was somewhat startling as there were partial and almost fully nude couples kissing, touching, and at one point even having sex. You couldn't see details, but it was still surprising to see that. After the video ended the professor asked what we thought the video was about and what human sexuality meant to us. Most students were reluctant to answer as I think that both the topic and video were uncomfortable for many.

Watching it definitely got me thinking about Tom a bit, wondering if maybe he would try to kiss me after coffee. I know that it was a bit presumptuous of me and maybe a little soon to think that considering I just met him and didn't really know anything about him, but he had this aura about him that I was very interested in.

After lunch I had a class before I was supposed to meet Tom and while I sat there making notes I felt my phone vibrating in my pocket. I pulled it out to see that Tom had sent me a text, "We still on for 2:00?" "Of course," I replied.

I couldn't help but smile as I was very smitten over this guy, yet I didn't really know anything about him. I anxiously watched the clock as my class came to an end, looking forward to seeing Tom. I briskly walked over to Books & Beans and when I walked in Tom was already waiting at a table. He stood up as I came towards him and gave a small wave with a smile. He offered to buy me a coffee for which I thanked him. We sat at a corner table of the coffee shop and started sharing our backgrounds a bit, what made us come to this school, and future career goals. He asked about my family, but didn't mention much when I asked about his. He kept wanting to know more about me, which made me feel like he was genuinely interested, but when I asked him questions about his personal life he somehow reverted back to questions about me. Other than that, our conversation flowed smoothly and he showed his sense of humor making me laugh several times.

As I had another class at three I had to be mindful of the time, but I was really enjoying our visit. We both had our hands on the table, and I couldn't help but notice his one hand was quite close to mine. Then while I was telling him about some of my hobbies like growing up playing sports, he ever so slightly moved his hand and gently grabbed my hand with a couple of fingers. I looked down at our hands and back up at him and smiled. I felt tingling in my legs. We continued to talk for another ten minutes or so and his fingers stayed locked into mine. I looked down at my phone and realized that I better get to class so Tom offered to walk with me. As we walked out of the coffee shop he put his hand on the small of my back and held the door open for me. As we reached the classroom, Tom told me what a great time he had and hoped we could see each other again soon. I told him I would like that. He leaned in and gave me a kiss on my cheek. I could feel myself turning a little red, but gave him a smile and turned to go into class so that it wasn't so obvious.

As I sat in my seat I still had butterflies in my stomach. I got settled and looked towards the door and I could see Tom smiling as he waved to me. I smiled back, then looked down to grab my laptop out of my bag and when I looked up he was gone. I said to myself before I came to college that I wouldn't get involved with anyone as I wanted to focus on my studies, and those were also my dad's words; there was just something about Tom that I couldn't stop thinking about him.

Soon after Jessica walked in and sat down beside me. "So, how did it go?" she asked with excitement.

"Good," I replied with a smile on my face, trying not to act like a giddy adolescent. She wanted more details, but the professor walked in to start the class. "I'll tell you later," I said to Jessica, and we turned our attention to the front of the room.

.

4

The Chase (The Train)

As I lay there feeling every ache on my body, trying to catch my breath and calm down a bit, I managed to pull myself up onto a bench. As I did, I could see blood smeared on the floor, which was most likely from my feet and some from my leg. I looked around and there was one guy sitting in the corner about thirty feet away, minding his own business.

He looked about fifty years old or so and had a medium build with some gray in his hair. I saw him look at me and I kept turning my eyes back to him to see if he was going to do anything. My guess is he was unsure whether to help me or leave me be as some people don't want to get involved in other people's situations.

After sitting there a few minutes, he asked "Are you okay?"

Trying to be strong, I wanted to say yes, but instead I started crying and shook my head and managed a faint "no".

"My name is Charlie, I can help you."

I sat there looking around and felt tears running down my face.

"We need to get you to a hospital."

I shook my head again.

"What happened to your leg?"

"I fell," I said quietly.

"Who did this to you?" I could hear concern in his voice.

I could feel myself trembling and as I started to answer, we heard a bang that sounded like it came from another part of the train. This was followed by another bang and then what sounded like a door opening. I thought we would have been at the next stop by now. Then as I heard a loud crash of thunder, the lights on the train flickered and when I turned my head to one of the doors of the cabin there was someone standing at the door. My heart started pounding. I didn't think he had got on the train when I rolled in. "How was that possible?" I thought to myself. Maybe we already stopped once and I hadn't noticed while I was talking with Charlie.

Charlie turned his head and saw the man as well. "Do you know him?" Charlie asked.

"Please help me!" I gasped. I felt the train slowing down. Charlie stood up and walked towards the door. He was waving his arms as if to tell the man to leave. The man persisted at trying to open the door while Charlie attempted to hold it shut. As I kept watching their inter-action, I could feel the train slowing down even more. I could see Charlie was struggling as the door flew open.

Charlie fell towards the side on a seat and the man was focused on me. "Charlie!" I screamed. Charlie leaped towards him, knocking him into one of the seats, and followed it up with a right hook. The man swung back at Charlie hitting him in the face and then kicked him back towards the seat across. Both men abruptly stood up and grappled, and I could see he was still focused on reaching me. The train felt as though it was just about to stop and I was near a door, frantically waiting for it to open. As the train shuddered to a halt, the man managed to shove Charlie back and was heading for me.

"Please, don't!" I begged.

As he got within about four feet from me, Charlie came running and threw himself into the man, tossing him a few feet past me onto the floor. The doors opened and just as I stepped out I looked at Charlie and mouthed "Thank you". As the doors shut in front of me I heard the train make the noise when it's ready to move again and saw Charlie standing at the window of the door.

Then just as it started moving again, the man came from behind him and Charlie's eyes went big and his mouth opened. It was like he couldn't move; then I saw it. A knife was sticking out of his back as the man had got up and stabbed Charlie. Charlie fell to the ground and the man stared at me with a cold look while the train slowly drifted away out of my sight.

I couldn't believe I had just seen him kill someone: that could have been me. I knew I didn't have long until the next stop as he would get off and continue to look for me so I had to get somewhere safe. I wasn't really sure where I was and there wasn't much around me except one little diner in the distance. By now the sun was starting to come up and so I hoped it was open. Maybe I could use a phone there and a bathroom to wash some of this blood off, and possibly find something to wrap my feet with as I could still feel glass pieces in them.

I limped towards the diner, exhausted and in pain, but this could be my only hope. I had to try and call Jessica, maybe she could come get me. The rain was still pouring but I made it to the diner. I noticed to the side of the diner there were washrooms, but figured I better go inside the restaurant first to try and call Jessica. I pushed open the door which was followed by a bell of some sort above me.

Looking around as I hobbled inside, there was nobody there except for one girl behind the counter, a cook in the back, and an older man sitting in a booth in the back corner of the restaurant.

"Do you have a phone?" I asked.

5

Dating Tom

After class, Jessica started prying about details of my coffee date with Tom. "So what did you guys talk about? What was he like? Did he try and kiss you?"

"Holy, what's with all questions?" I chuckled.

"Hey, you're the first one to have a guy interested, so I'm going to live vicariously for now," she replied.

"Fair enough," I said with a smile back. "He was interesting and sweet. He asked about my life a lot and didn't talk too much about himself. I have to admit he did look good in his jeans and fitted shirt. We talked about interests and family, mostly mine, but he was very easy to talk to. He gently grabbed my hand about halfway through and I didn't resist. Then I had to go to my next class."

"And?" Jessica asked, as if knowing I had left out some details.

"And what?"

"Did he try and kiss you?" she demanded with a smile.

"Actually he was a gentleman, but he did lean in to kiss my cheek." I smiled again. Jessica's eyes lit up after hearing that.

"You are in trouble, girl. I can see you are into him. Just don't go jumping in too fast. You have four years at this college and there are a lot of guys here."

"You sound like my dad," I replied with a snicker.

That night I stayed in my dorm room to get some homework done. I couldn't help but think about Tom as we had had a great coffee date and there was something about him that intrigued me. I thought I would take the initiative and send him a text as he was usually the one texting me, but I didn't want to sound too eager.

"Hey Tom, it's me. Just wanted to say hi. I enjoyed our coffee today."

Within seconds I saw he had read my text and was writing me back.

"I'm glad you texted me. I was just thinking about you and enjoyed our time together too. I hope you didn't mind me kissing your cheek or think I was too forward?"

Reading his text I couldn't help but smile and even felt butterflies.

"No I didn't mind," I replied. "Well I better get back to studying. I have a quiz tomorrow."

"Okay, look forward to seeing you soon," he responded, adding a smiling emoji. "Sleep tight," he sent.

"Goodnight Tom," I sent back. Then I hit the books for another hour and fell asleep.

The next morning I stopped at Books and Beans to grab a coffee to take to my class. While I was standing in line about to pay, I heard a voice say "I'll get that".

I turned and it was Tom. I was a little surprised that he was there the same time as me, but I didn't read anything into it and I was happy to see him.

"Thanks," I said with a smile.

"Mind if I walk you to class?" he asked.

"Not at all," I replied, still smiling.

We chatted while walking to class and he wished me good luck on my test.

"Thanks," I said. I was impressed as it showed he was listening to me last night. Most guys just pretend to listen because they are after one thing.

Jessica walked into class shortly after me and sat down beside me. "Where did you go this morning?" I asked her.

"Went for a morning jog. I try to go most mornings if I don't sleep in."

"So guess who surprised me at the coffee shop this morning?"

"Tom?" She guessed with a smile.

"Yup. I was standing in line and, as I was paying, I heard him tell the guy at the counter that he would pay. I was surprised, but in a good way."

"So he just happened to be there when you were?" she asked with a touch of concern.

"Stop reading into it," I responded, "I thought it was sweet."

"Okay, okay, but don't say I didn't warn you" she muttered back.

"Oh you're being silly. It's not like that." I replied.

Our professor came in right then and announced our test was about to begin and to put all phones and laptops away.

As I wrote my test I felt pretty confident in my answers, but I also caught myself drifting in thought a few times. Jessica made me wonder why Tom had been at the coffee shop this morning, but then I thought she was reading into it and would focus back on my test. I didn't want her negative thoughts ruining what I thought was a sweet gesture from Tom.

I finished before Jessica so I waited outside the lecture theatre for her. As I stood there checking my phone, I heard someone say "So did you find the test easy?" I looked up and there was a guy standing somewhat in front of me. I responded by saying "Yeah, I thought it was pretty easy."

He introduced himself as Calvin. He said he had noticed me in class the other day and thought he would say hi. "I'm Kerry," I said and extended my hand to shake his. He wasn't as sexy and handsome as Tom, but he was cute in a plain kind of way. We talked about other classes we both had and he mentioned where he was from.

About fifteen minutes later Jessica came out. I introduced her to Calvin and we all had the same class together next so we walked to the building, chatting about college so far and campus life. We sat down together in the middle of the lecture hall with me in the middle and Jessica on my left and Calvin on my right. Calvin kept talking to me, asking where I came from and about my family. He seemed genuine and was a really nice guy. He even made me laugh a few times. The class was quite full and I checked the time to see if class was starting soon and noticed I had a text message from Tom.

"Hey, we have this class together. Just walked in, but noticed there were no seats near you. Too bad." He added a sad face emoji.

I looked around briefly, but couldn't see him.

"Where are you sitting?" I texted back.

"In the back," he replied.

"Who's that sitting beside you?"

"Some guy we met from our other class. His name is Calvin."

"Oh," he sent back.

"Well, class is going to start, but maybe we can grab a bite after?"

"Sure," he replied.

"K, talk after," I said.

I leaned over to Jessica and whispered, "Tom's here."

Her eyes opened wide and she whispered, "Where? Why?"

"He has this class, he said."

"Really?" Jessica responded doubtfully.

"Oh stop, I know what you're thinking, but he told me he was doing psychology courses as a psych minor in his business degree so we are bound to have a few classes together."

"I'm just saying." she replied.

The professor walked in and class started. During class, Calvin leaned in a couple of times to ask me about what Jessica and I were doing this weekend and if we knew about any parties coming up. I responded briefly as I was trying to pay attention to the professor but didn't want to be rude to Calvin.

I looked behind me a couple of times and I finally noticed Tom in the back. The first time I looked back he didn't see me, but the second time he was looking at me and I gave him a smile when I looked back.

After class Tom was waiting in the hall for us and asked if we were going to lunch. Jessica jumped in and responded by saying "That sounds like a great idea," and invited Calvin as well. "You don't mind Tom, do you?" I asked.

He looked at Calvin and then back at me, "No, not a problem," he replied, but I could tell he wasn't overly enthusiastic.

At lunch we had a good conversation and Tom even talked to Calvin so I figured he was fine with him being there. As we finished up lunch we chatted about the upcoming weekend. There was supposed to be a couple of parties and also some sort of event at the Pool Shark. Jessica and I mentioned we would probably head to the Pool Shark as we weren't really into the frat parties at this point, but that might change after we had done our sorority initiation. The guys both said they would likely see us there, to which we both smiled and gave them an approximate time we would be there. We exchanged numbers with Calvin so we could get in touch if we needed to and I already had Tom's number.

Jessica and I walked to our next class together and I asked her what she thought of Calvin. She said she thought he was cute and sweet, but she also thought he might be into me instead. I reassured her I wasn't interested as I liked Tom and wanted to see where that went and gave her my approval to go after Calvin if she wanted to.

As we sat in class I felt my phone buzz in my pocket. I carefully pulled it out, and to my surprise I had a text from Calvin. "Thanks for inviting me to lunch, it was nice meeting you and your friend Jessica. Maybe I will see you guys this Friday at the Pool Shark."

"It was nice meeting you too," I replied. I figured I had better say something to show him I was not into him that way and for Jessica's sake so I sent another text.

"I think my friend likes you."

"Really?"

"Yeah, she told me you were cute and really sweet, but don't tell her I told you, lol. What do you think of her?"

"That's cool. She's attractive for sure and she seems like an awesome girl," he replied.

"You should come Friday and I'll make sure she's there. I think you guys would hit it off!"

"Okay, I'll come around 8. See you then."

"Sounds good," I replied and added a smiley face.

Jessica leaned over and said "Who're you texting? Let me guess, Tom?"

"No, actually it was Calvin."

"See, I knew he was into you more," she replied.

"Actually I told him you thought he was cute and he said you were attractive and seemed like a great girl."

She was somewhat bothered I had told him that, but in a cute way, not actually mad.

"He's going to come Friday and meet up with us."

Jessica blushed as she smiled.

"We can double date," I said. I smiled and we focused back on the professor.

After our last class, Jessica and I grabbed a quick bite at one of the fast food joints on campus and then headed back to the dorm. Jessica mentioned she was going to go for a walk, but I told her I was going to stay in as I had an assignment and test coming up, and although I was spending time with Tom, I wanted to make sure I kept up on my studies. My dad had also sent me a text earlier letting me know he was thinking about me and asking how school was going. I let him know things were going well and that I missed him. We generally texted or talked daily: I realized it was hard on him not having his little girl around the house anymore and I admittedly missed hanging out with him too as we had always had a special bond growing up.

I had probably been studying in my room for about two hours when my phone buzzed. I was kind of wondering where Jessica was as she never mentioned specifically where she was going after we ate, she just said she had to be somewhere and left abruptly.

"Hey girl, sorry I left so quickly, but I went to Books & Beans to see about getting a part-time job as I could really use the money. I didn't tell you because I didn't want to say anything unless I actually got the job. Then I went for a yoga class. I shouldn't be too long."

"No worries," I replied.

"How did the interview go?"

"Great! I start next week. You should get a job here too as they are looking for extra help still."

"Maybe a little extra cash would be nice," I responded.

"Awesome! I can let my new boss know you are interested."

"Sounds good, talk soon. Have to get back to studying."

"K, see you soon," Jessica replied.

As I just got back into my books, my phone buzzed again. I need to start turning this thing off when studying, I thought to myself.

"Hey cutie," Tom's text read.

"Hey, what's up?" I replied. I couldn't help but smile.

"Just thinking about you and wondering what you were doing."

"Studying," and I added a sad emoji face.

"Looking forward to seeing you Friday," Tom said.

"Me too. I should get back to the books though. Talk tomorrow?"

"Okay, night."

My eyes were getting very heavy so I figured any extra studying at this point would just be information going in without any retention. I crawled under the covers and must have been out within minutes because I didn't even hear Jessica come in.

The next morning I was running a little late for class so I didn't have time to stop for a coffee, but to my surprise Tom was waiting for me by my class with a coffee in hand for me. I thought that was so sweet of him and gave him a kiss on the cheek and thanked him. I apologized for not being able to talk longer as I had to get into class, but he didn't seem to mind.

Once I sat down I texted him, thanking him again and sent a kiss emoji. He was so sweet and each day I saw him my feelings were getting stronger. I also texted him saying I couldn't wait to hang out at the Pool Shark. He replied that he was really looking forward to spending some quality time with me. I couldn't help but smile.

I met up with Jessica at lunch as she wanted to meet and discuss plans for tomorrow night, what to wear, and her thoughts on Calvin. She also told me to make sure and get up early tomorrow so we could get to Books and Beans and talk to the manager about a job for me. I agreed to wake up earlier as I knew she put in a good word for me.

That night I figured I better put a little more effort into my studies as the past couple nights were not as productive as I would have liked and I wanted to relax this weekend and spend some time with Tom. Jessica and I decided to go to the library to study because we had never been inside before and wanted to see what the library was like on campus, plus it would help avoid the temptation to just go to bed if we were in our rooms. We studied for a good couple of hours before heading back to our dorm and I felt like I was productive so I could enjoy the weekend.

The next morning we made it to the coffee shop in plenty of time to talk to Jason, the manager. He was really nice and took about 10 minutes to sit with me and basically interview me in a non-formal way right there. He seemed pleased with my responses and asked when I could start. I could see Jessica smiling in the background as she must have overheard him. I tried not to smile back so he wouldn't think she was listening or that I wasn't paying attention to him.

"I could start next week," I replied.

He was good with that and brought out some paperwork for me to fill out.

"I guess I will see you Monday afternoon," I replied.

"Grab a coffee for yourself on your way out," he kindly responded.

Another benefit of working here is I get free coffee and I LOVE my morning coffee.

Jessica joined me in the line and grabbed my arm, squeezing it with excitement that we got to work together. I was pretty excited too.

Once we had our coffee, we headed to class. It was a long day for me as I had a full day of classes without spares, but I kept thinking about our double date tonight with Tom and Calvin which helped me get through the day. Jessica and I had last block together so once the bell rang, we headed back to our room to get ready for the evening. I could tell she was starting to get a little excited about seeing Calvin and of course I was feeling anxious about seeing Tom as I hadn't seen him in a couple of days.

It was getting close to 7 p.m. so we figured we had better head to the pub to meet the boys and just before we left I received a text from Tom, "Can't wait to see you."

"Me too," I replied.

Jessica and I arrived first so we grabbed a table and ordered water while we waited. About 20 minutes later, in walked Tom with a big smile as soon as he saw me. He came right up to me and hugged me while lifting me off my feet. Then he grabbed my cheeks, looked me in the eyes, and kissed my forehead gently. I was somewhat surprised by his forwardness, especially in public, but I didn't mind; I actually liked that he did that. Admittedly

I hoped he would have kissed my lips. I looked down at Jessica sitting in the booth and her eyebrows were raised and she was smiling as if to say she was happy for me. He asked Jessica and me what we wanted to drink and ordered for all of us, which I thought was a nice gesture.

A couple minutes later Calvin walked in and you could tell he was a bit nervous, but he said hi to Jessica and extended his arm to shake her hand. She smiled back and then they sat down in the booth with Tom and me. The conversation flowed casually between the four of us. We talked about school, sports, family, and campus life. Even Tom and Calvin seemed to be getting along. I don't really know how many drinks we had, but I was definitely starting to feel it so I told Tom I had better slow down and have water for a while. He was a gentleman and had the server bring over a pitcher of water. I thought maybe he would have somewhat encouraged me to continue drinking or think I wasn't fun, but he supported me and it was then that I knew my feelings for him were very real. The four of us played pool and darts and even sang some karaoke at one point, which made for great laughs because none of us were really singers, but we had fun.

It started to get late and I told Jessica I would be heading back to the room but she wanted to stay a bit longer with Calvin. Tom offered to walk me back to my dorm so I happily accepted. He grabbed my hand while we walked and I could feel butterflies in my stomach. We laughed about the karaoke and our pool skills and as we got close to my dorm Tom told me how great a time he had with me. As we arrived at my door, he wrapped his arms around me, kissed my forehead and looked into my eyes.

"I really like you, Kerry. You are like no one I have ever met before and I am falling hard for you."

I bit my lip to contain my emotions while hearing him say such words. "I really like you too," I replied with a smile.

Then he leaned in and kissed me so softly, but with a passion I could feel throughout my body. We must have kissed for a few minutes, but it felt like time stood still in that moment.

As our lips pulled away from one another, I smiled and said inquisitively, "I hope I can see you tomorrow?"

"Definitely. Maybe I can take you out for dinner?" he answered.

"Sounds great!" I replied.

I walked into the building and gave a cute little wave as I closed the door. I got ready for bed and just as I slid under the cover my phone made the noise it makes when I get a text.

"I had a great time tonight with you!"

"Me too," I texted back.

"BTW, I love kissing you," Tom replied.

I answered with a blushing emoji, "Night."

"Goodnight," Tom replied once more.

As I lay there, I started to wonder where Jessica was. I hoped they had hit it off because then we could double date and Tom would see that Calvin was into Jessica and not me. He doesn't seem like the overly jealous type, and it's kind of cute that he was worried some other guy was interested in me. I take it as a sign he must like me enough to care.

About ten minutes later Jessica walked in and she was smiling from ear to ear.

"Look at you, all giddy and happy. So how did it go?" I asked.

"He's a great guy Kerry, I really like him."

"That's amazing. I'm so happy for you!" I replied.

"He even kissed me before I came inside."

"Wow. You don't waste any time," I said smiling back at her.

She proceeded to tell me about their night and conversation and I also told her about the rest of Tom's and my night. We must have talked for almost another hour, but my eyes started to get heavy so I told Jess I was going to hit the sack.

The next morning Jessica and I were woken bright and early to the sound of banging pots and girls rushing into our room, yelling at us to get out of bed. We were actually a bit scared as we didn't know that the hell was going on and then one girl yelled, "It's initiation time, bitches!" We were told we had two minutes to be downstairs in the lobby of our dorm so we didn't even get to put different clothes on – good thing I didn't sleep naked. As we got downstairs there were about ten other girls there, all of whom seemed to be freshmen waiting for this initiation and not thrilled about it either.

We stood there for about ten minutes when another girl came down the stairs, holding a paddle. To my dismay, it was Brittany. At that moment, I remembered her mentioning initiation in the showers, but hadn't thought that she was the one doing it. "Just great," I thought to myself. She walked down the line looking at all of us, then stopped in front of me, looked me up and down and said, "This is going to be fun," in a smirking tone. "Phase one, ladies, bend over and get ready to get paddled. If you flinch, cry out, or even move, you will get it twice," she ordered. One by one she went through the line and walloped each girl's backside. Some girls teared up, but tried not to show it.

"Phase two. We will be drawing something on your face. It is not to be removed for the entire weekend. If it is removed and you are seen without it before the end of the weekend, you will be out of the sorority.

Brittany and another girl proceeded to draw on each girl's face with black marker: some got nasty words like "whore" and "deep throater", while others got drawings. Of course Brittany did mine and as she approached me and went to write on me, I swatted her hand away. She gave me a nasty look and suggested I keep my hands to myself or it would not be good for me. She continued to write and once she was done, she had a smug smile on her face. I turned to Jessica to ask what she had written and she told me I had 'virgin' written across my forehead. Although I was proud of actually being one, I didn't appreciate advertising it on my face for everyone to see.

"Final stage, girls. Let's go outside." Once we had all moved out to the front lawn, embarrassed as others walked by, Brittany spoke up saying that we were all going to get hosed with cold water for 20 seconds. If we so much as moved or turned our heads, we would be out. I was at least happy I had worn shorts and a decent t-shirt to bed, as some girls were in just a bra and underwear and were already shivering. There was a large barrel of water with a hose attached and Brittany went down the line soaking each girl, one by one, from head to toe with freezing cold water.

One of the girls in her underwear turned her body and moved away from her spot and she was told to leave. She was out of the sorority. Another girl got sprayed in the mouth so much that she started coughing and moved off of her spot and was also kicked out. Jessica took it like a trouper and didn't move and I was next. I was not about to give Brittany the satisfaction of beating me. She started by spraying me right in my chest, hoping this would make me move and then went up to my face. It was cold as hell but I kept my eyes shut and went to a different place in my mind to overcome the pain of the cold and pressure hitting my face. I couldn't see the time, but it sure felt like more than twenty seconds to me. She probably went longer just to try and get me out. Then the water stopped. I opened my eyes and she gave me a brief look, almost as if she was impressed, but equally annoyed that I hadn't moved.

"You're not getting rid of me that easy, bitch", I thought. We were then told we had to wait outside, soaking wet, freezing, and most of us in our pajamas or less for an hour before we were able to go back in. Monday morning if we had completed the task of keeping our face drawings, we would receive something letting us know we had made the sorority.

It was a long hour, but we all made it and went back into the dorm to have a hot shower and change into dry clothes. When I got out of the shower, I checked my phone and noticed that Tom had texted me. He had a great place he was going to take me for dinner, but wanted to keep it a surprise. I didn't mind as I kind of like surprises and it made it exciting knowing he was taking the initiative. I was a little nervous because I had that stupid word on my forehead and this was our actual first date. We had seen each other a fair bit and went to the pub together, but this was kind of our official first date and I wanted everything to go right.

Jessica helped me get ready by doing my hair for me and helped me pick out an outfit, and even tried to use my hair to cover up the word. I didn't want to be kicked out of the sorority, but I definitely couldn't go out to a restaurant like this, so I figured I would wash it off and then have Jessica draw it back on after my date. Thankfully it was able to come off, but it took a lot of scrubbing and my forehead was a little red, however it was better than what was on there. As I finished up getting ready, I couldn't help but think about my dad's words to me, telling me to focus on school and not boys, but you can't help who you meet and there was just something about Tom that had me feeling like this could really be something special. Plus, I was an adult now and could take care of myself and make my own decisions.

I texted Tom to confirm what time he would be picking me up, to which he responded shortly after saying he would be there in about an hour. I answered with a smiley face and told him that worked. Before I knew it he arrived, texting me while standing outside my dorm building. Even though I had been seeing him for a bit now, I still got butterflies knowing I was about to go on this date. I opened the door to him smiling, while holding a single rose which he handed me followed by a gentle kiss.

"You look beautiful," he said intently.

"Thank you," I said with a smile.

"We should go as I have reservations for 8:00," Tom said.

"Okay, I'm excited" I replied, not trying to sound too giddy.

As we drove to the unknown place to me, Tom put his hand on my thigh and I put my hand on top of his. We talked about all kinds of things and the conversation was just so natural. I felt like I had known him for a long time. We pulled into this large building with a parking garage so I still didn't really know where we were going. He proved himself to be a gentleman by opening my car door for me, helping me out, and offering his arm as we walked to the door to the building. As we went into the elevator, he asked me to close my eyes and without hesitation I did. He whispered in my ear, "Do you trust me?"

"I do," I whispered back. Then he leaned in and kissed me sensually and as he stopped he asked me to keep my eyes closed. The elevator stopped and he helped me out of the elevator and walk what felt like about 10-15 feet. "Okay, open your eyes", he instructed. As I opened my eyes, there in front of me was this beautiful restaurant and in the background all I could see were windows and the skyline of the city. He had taken me to a new revolving restaurant on the 50th floor of a hotel. It was breathtaking and I couldn't stop smiling. He had reserved a table right by a massive window so we had the best view. He proceeded to inform me that this restaurant did a full 360 view of the city over the course of an hour.

We ordered wine and had a four-course meal with some of the most amazing food I had ever tasted. We laughed and had deep conversations. I even told him about the initiation earlier that morning and how I couldn't stand that Brittany chick. He told me he felt bad for me and that if he ever met her, she might get a taste of her own medicine. I laughed and told him how she was one of those girls that throws herself at guys and thinks she can always get her way. Then I tried to change the topic as I didn't want to bring the mood down.

While waiting for dessert, he gazed at me, not saying a word, just smiling. I asked him what he was thinking, and then he said, "You are the most amazing girl I have ever met and I feel so lucky to have found you." In that moment, I could feel myself falling in love with him. I know it was fairly quick, but I couldn't help it. He was everything I could ever want: he was kind, sensitive, thoughtful, attractive, driven, passionate, funny, and he wanted me. How did I get so lucky?

After we finished dinner, we walked back to the parking garage hand-in-hand and as we got to the car, before he opened the door for me, he gently pushed me up against the car and gave me another passionate kiss. This time, Tom started to slide his hand under my dress and I didn't mind at all. I was totally lost in the moment and could feel his hand rubbing me and how wet I was. About two minutes later we heard the door in the parking garage open so that ended our moment, and we both laughed about it as we got into the car. As we drove back to the dorm I kept thinking about the intensity in the parking garage and how I wanted him to continue. I thought about my virginity and how I wanted to wait for marriage, or at least the person I felt I was truly in love with, and I think Tom could be that person. This was a feeling unlike any I had ever experienced, which made me feel like I was ready to take that step with him.

As he walked me up to my dorm building I stopped him and thanked him for the best time I had ever had. He said he should thank me for being such a good date and then I just smiled and leaned in for another kiss. Then I leaned in and whispered in his ear, "I think I am falling for you," to which he smiled and whispered back in my

ear, "me too". We kissed once more and just as I was about to walk away, he gently grabbed my arm and pulled me towards him. Then he said something I wasn't expecting: "I want you to be my girlfriend, exclusively." I smiled and said "I'd like that," then I turned and walked inside.

When I got up to the room, Jessica was waiting up for me so that I could tell her all the details. She was smiling the entire time I was talking and then when I told her I thought I was falling in love with him, her mouth opened, somewhat in shock, but in a good way and she told me how happy she was for me.

She told me that she wasn't at that point with Calvin yet, but that she could definitely see something with him. By now it was quite late so we both decided to go to bed. As I lay there I couldn't help but still feel giddy from the amazing date and that he had asked me to be his girlfriend. I could definitely see this turning into something long term; he seemed perfect.

That Sunday night, we had two girls come bursting into our room, yelling at us to stand at attention at once. They were there to check on our face drawings to ensure we had adhered to the rules. Thankfully I had remembered to ask Jessica to draw mine back on and Jessica's was still visible as she hadn't really left the dorm for the past thirty hours to avoid embarrassment. After they quickly inspected us, they left and went on to the next rooms. The next morning we heard a knock at our door and Jessica opened it. There was a package with both our names on it. Inside were t-shirts and hoodies with the sorority symbols and 'BFL' and 'Bitches For Life' below it. There was also a note that read, "Congrats on joining our sorority." Jessica and I looked at each other. "We're in!" we shrieked and hugged each other. "Maybe now that Brittany chick will get off my back," I thought to myself.

6

Dating Tom Part II

Over the following year, Tom and I saw each other pretty much every day; most mornings we grabbed a coffee together and walked to class. Sometimes our timetables aligned so we could have lunch together, and then usually saw each other a couple of nights during the week and spent most of the weekend together. We would go to the movies, parties on campus, shopping, and often went to the Pool Shark as we didn't have to drive, enjoyed the atmosphere, and started to get to know other students and make new friends. I also worked at the coffee shop a couple of days each week so that kept me busy, but Tom would sometimes come in and study while having a coffee. We would exchange cute smiles and I would go chat with him when it was a little slow. We also hung out with Jessica and Calvin a lot too and Tom seemed to even become friends with Calvin. Everything seemed so perfect between us and Tom continued to be the gentleman and sweetheart I fell for.

I did come across Brittany, occasionally, some mornings in the girls shower area and we saw her fairly regularly at the Pool Shark. I also served her coffee a few times when she happened to come in during my shift. One morning she was in the coffee shop and I brought coffee to her table. I detected that same orange smell that came from the dorm room next to mine from time to time. I never did see her come out of the room, only another girl, but it made me start to wonder if she was living there too. I never tried knocking on that door because most of the time she was such a bitch that I didn't want anything to do with her.

Anyways, she still had this attitude about her that came across like she was better than everybody else. She was a bit more pleasant to me since I was in the sorority, but I still think she had a problem with me, or maybe it was something of mine that she wanted. She would greet Tom when she saw us together and he generally reciprocated, but I knew I didn't have to worry about him as he was a loyal and genuine guy who only had eyes for me. There was just something about her I didn't trust.

Tom's and my anniversary was coming up and I had been wanting to tell him I was in love with him for a while, but I thought with this special occasion coming up it would make it more special to wait. We also hadn't had sex yet as I really wanted to be sure before I gave myself fully to him. This didn't mean I didn't think about it a lot, and we had done other stuff to be intimate, but taking that final step was something I didn't take lightly and only wanted to give to one person. I knew I loved Tom and wanted it to be with him and planned to give myself to him on our anniversary.

Tom would text me every second day, reminding me about our big day coming up and asking me whether I wanted it to be a surprise or not. I told him I liked surprises but if he wanted to tell me I would be okay with that too. "A surprise it is", he texted me. I just replied with a smiley face. The weekend was the big day and he told me to not make any plans. "As if I would," I thought: I had been looking forward to this for quite a while. He picked me up in his car and we drove to a place that seemed familiar, although I wasn't fully sure as he had blindfolded me. We got into an elevator and when it stopped, he helped me out. He took my arm and helped me walk a short distance and then told me to slide off my blindfold. We were at the same restaurant we had had our first date. He even managed to get the same table. I thought it was romantic.

Halfway through dinner, he slipped me an invitation that read, "To my sweet Kerry, I can't believe a guy like me was so lucky to have found a girl like you. You make my world better in so many ways and I know when I look into your eyes, you are the one I love. I don't want this special day to end. Instead I want to wake up with you tomorrow morning. Would you spend the night with me?"

My eyes were a bit watery from the beautiful words he wrote, and I also recognized that he had told me he loved me in the letter. "You love me?" I asked.

"100%," he replied.

I was at a loss for words. He wanted to spend the night together, which likely meant he was expecting to have sex, but hearing his words gave me confirmation that I wanted to spend the night with him too.

About a minute went by and then I replied "Tom, you make me feel something I never thought I would feel and I feel so special and safe when I am with you. I love you too!" My body was tingling and it felt so good telling him finally. He asked if I wanted to head up to our hotel room he booked for us and I smiled and nodded.

As we walked to the room, he put his hand around my waist and I could even feel him slightly touching the top part of my ass as well and I started to get butterflies. As we approached the door and he was about to open it, he turned to me and kissed me intently. He turned my back to the door and leaned up against me kissing me more intensely. He managed to open the door with his key while still kissing me. As the door shut behind us we separated briefly, but then he turned back towards me and pulled his jacket off and took me in his arms. We continued kissing passionately while we walked towards the bed and we both fell down on top of the covers. I paused briefly and asked him to give me a couple minutes while I went to the bathroom.

I wanted to freshen up if we were going to be intimate, but I also thought it was sensual to have a shower together so I started the shower and shortly after, I asked him to come see me. He came into the washroom and saw me in the shower and I said, "well, aren't you going to join me"?

It didn't take long for him to come in and he took one look at me standing there with water running down my body and he grabbed me in his arms and started kissing me. We had our hands all over each other as we kissed and my body was quivering as I wanted him so bad. He kissed me all over and even went down on me and gave me an orgasm I never felt before. Shortly after, I told him I wanted to go to the bed so he picked me up, carried me to the bed, and gently laid me down. I took one look into his eyes and he asked me, "Are you sure you're ready?" I nodded and bit my bottom lip.

He slowly started to kiss me and moved his body on top of mine. I could feel every part of him on me and I wanted him to make love to me. Then I felt him slowly go inside me and although it hurt a bit, it felt so good and I wanted him to continue. Our bodies moved together like two puzzle pieces, as we kissed and touched each other all over. I could feel myself getting close and I didn't hold back. As we both climaxed, we looked at one another and could feel our bodies shiver with intensity. It was the most amazing feeling I had ever had.

We lay there for about an hour, talking and cuddling after and I thanked him for the best anniversary and evening anyone could ask for. He told me there was one more thing. He got up, went into his bag and pulled out a gift. I wasn't expecting anything because we had talked about not getting gifts so I didn't get him anything except a nice picture of us in a frame.

I opened the gift and it was a beautiful necklace with 'TK' on it, for Tom & Kerry. I was elated and loved the gift, so much so that I showed him my gratitude with another round of love-making. Shortly after that, we fell asleep in each other's arms.

The next morning I woke up, but Tom was already out of bed. I could hear the shower running and then the door knock. I answered the door and it was room service. Tom had surprised me with breakfast in bed. I told him it arrived so he quickly got out of the shower, dried off, and came out to join me.

"Did you have a good night?" he asked.

"It was pretty good," I said with a smile.

"I'm glad," he replied. "Me too."

After breakfast we got dressed and checked out of the hotel. I told Tom on the way back to the campus that I had a big test on Monday so I needed to do some studying. He was understanding and dropped me off at the dorm. I thanked him again for everything and gave him a kiss goodbye.

"Talk later?" I said.

"You bet," he replied.

I walked into the building and up to my room. As I walked toward my room, I saw a girl with brown hair going into the room beside mine. Was that Brittany? I guess it didn't matter if it was, but I was kind of curious because this was the girl who was somewhat annoyed with me and thought she was all that and she seemed to be living right next to me. Any other time I would have knocked on the door to see, but I was thinking about Tom and studying so I just went to my own room.

As I got ready for bed I happened to bump the picture on my wall, causing it to swing to the side and to my surprise there was a decent-sized hole in the wall. Normally I would have just moved the picture back, but I could hear sounds coming through the hole: sounds that I had never heard before with the picture blocking the hole. I didn't want to be someone who spies but my curiosity got the better of me and I had to look. I could see the edge of the bed so it must have been close to the wall and a little further back, I could see two girls talking by a desk. One was blonde and the other looked like the brunette girl who I had seen enter the room a couple of minutes earlier. I couldn't quite make out her face as the hole wasn't that big and they were on the other side of the room. I could faintly hear them talking and they mentioned something about meeting some guys at the Pool Shark or something. I then saw one girl walk towards the bed and I quickly slid the picture back in case they could see anything through the hole. The hole must have never been patched as it wouldn't appear to be all the way through the wall if someone on that side looked at it because the picture blocked it. I was so intrigued to find out if that was in fact Brittany that I would try to sneak a peek fairly often when I was in my room. Sometimes the room was empty but other times I could hear them: I never managed to get a complete view of the brunette. A few weeks went by and one night, while I was supposed to be studying, I looked through the hole and there she was. It was Brittany and she was talking to her roommate. She mentioned how she had been talking to this cute guy, but half of the conversation was still a little muffled. I heard something about chatting with him at the coffee shop, but then I heard her say "Too bad he has a girlfriend but hey, that's never stopped me before." She couldn't be talking about Tom, could she? Even if they did talk, I trusted him. Her? That's a totally different story.

Naturally my curiosity about the situation got the better of me and I figured I would ask Tom if he had spoken with this bimbo. I didn't plan to interrogate him, but figured I should know. So I called him and he admitted to chatting with some girl who came up to his table the other day. She had introduced herself as Brittany and said she had seen him often around campus. She told him that she had only said 'hi' before but now she wanted to talk to him. He told me how he was polite but had told her, in no uncertain terms, that he had a girlfriend. This relieved me to some extent, but I knew this girl's reputation and I wasn't going to let her get in the way of Tom and me.

About a week later, Tom, Calvin, Jessica and I were at the Pool Shark when Jessica nudged my arm and pointed toward the bar. It was Brittany and she was looking in our direction, at Tom. We were almost done our drinks so I volunteered to go get another round from the bar.

As I waited for my drinks, Brittany turned to me and said "Hi," upbeat and friendly.

"I don't know what you're intentions are but Tom and I are in a relationship so just find someone else to screw,"

I said to her in a low voice, tinged with hostility. I then grabbed the drinks and walked back to our table. Tom could sense I was a little wound up and asked me what was wrong. "I don't like that bitch; I know her type."

"You have nothing to worry about," he replied. "She just talked to me because she's seen me around campus." About thirty minutes later we were playing pool. Actually Jessica and I were perched on bar stools, watching the boys play. Brittany walked by the pool table, putting her hand on his shoulder as she walked by and softly said, "Good to see you again". He somewhat smiled back with a closed mouth, but I could sense the awkwardness as he knew I didn't like her. I was furious and told Jessica I was leaving and she said she would come with me. I told Tom I was leaving and he asked me to stay, but I was too upset. He and Calvin continued playing pool while Jessica and I left to walk back to our room.

Jessica tried to comfort me and tell me there was nothing to worry about, but I knew girls like Brittany and told her that Tom was the best thing to happen to me and I didn't want to lose him. She reassured me that Tom was a good guy and would never do anything to hurt me. I texted him about 30 minutes later, apologizing for leaving that way. He texted back that he understood and apologized that I was hurt by the situation and Brittany's flirting, but told me that he loved me and said we could talk tomorrow and not to wait up for him as he was going to stay and hang with Calvin a bit longer. I wasn't overly happy about that knowing Brittany was there, but I trusted him and was too tired to go back.

That week I was pretty busy with schoolwork and working at the coffee shop so I didn't see much of Tom, except for a couple of mornings for coffee and one night we went for ice cream. Things were still great between us, but he was a little distant. I continued to try and spy on Brittany through my hole in the wall and see what she was up to, but often her room was empty. That Saturday I didn't feel like going out as I had a big final coming up on Monday and so I told Tom I really needed to focus that weekend. He understood as I needed to do well in my studies to get into the placement I wanted. While studying, I thought I would take the odd break to look through my secret hole and the first few times I saw nothing, but around midnight I thought I would check once more and I saw two people, but this time one was a guy.

I thought it was very odd because guys weren't allowed in the dorm. I couldn't make out who it was but the two were laughing and standing quite close. I admit that part of me thought it could be Tom, but then I knew in my gut that he wouldn't do that to me. I thought I would just give a call to see if he was up, or at worst, hear his phone ring through the wall. It went straight to voicemail which it often did at night because he turned it off when he went to bed. As I turned to look back through the wall, the two people were standing right in front of the bed but I couldn't see their faces. Clothes started coming off and I saw them fall towards the bed, but again no faces. I focused on trying to see anything that resembled my Tom, even though I didn't want to believe it if it were true.

At one point I did see what looked like Brittany's face but I could only see the brown hair of the guy she was fooling around with. They continued and I listened until they both finished. My stomach was in knots as a part of me worried it was him, but I couldn't tell. I heard her say to him that he had better go before someone found him in the dorm. He jumped up and got dressed but I still couldn't see his face. As he walked to the door, I moved the picture back and tried to get up quickly to go to the door to catch this guy leaving her room. By the time I opened the door and looked out, all I saw was a tall guy with brown hair at the end of the hall. It couldn't have been Tom, could it?

The next morning I texted him to see what he had done last night and he said he had just stayed in and watched a movie and then had gone to bed early. I couldn't tell him about the hole in the wall as I didn't want to come across as a creepy nutcase who spied on her neighbors. So I just accepted what he said and went about my day.

The next few weeks Tom and I hung out regularly and talked about summer plans. He thought we should go on a road trip, to which I agreed. I only had a couple of years left in school and then would be starting my career and likely not have much time for road trips. Even next semester, I would be starting to work with clients so I was excited about that.

About a month later, just before summer break, I was in the girls' shower getting ready for classes when I heard some girls walk in. I heard one girl call Brittany's name so I decided to stay where I was and not come out. They were chatting about summer plans and all the boys they had met during the year. Brittany then said something to her friends that I would never forget.

"Remember last month when I had that guy over to my dorm room. It was the best sex ever. We texted back and forth and hopefully I'll get to see him some more this summer. I wish he would dump that girlfriend of his already. He needs a real woman, not some inexperienced coffee shop girl."

My stomach dropped as it was then that I was more certain that it was Tom. Why would he do that to me? I thought he was different, I said to myself. Once they had left, I gathered myself and went back to my room, skipping my next class. I texted him and said "How could you do this to me? I thought you loved me?"

He replied, "I don't know what you're talking about."

"You slept with Brittany!" I texted back.

"Kerry, I swear I didn't. You know me."

"How do I know you're telling me the truth?"

"You'll just have to trust me. I promise you. I didn't sleep with her," he responded.

"I just need some time to think. I'll text you later."

"Okay. I love you," he texted.

I didn't know what to believe at this point. I wanted to believe Tom but who else could Brittany be talking about. Calvin maybe? The way she looked at Tom and the few interactions they had had, it seemed possible it was Tom, but he was telling me it wasn't him and the only other girl from the coffee shop with a boyfriend was Jessica. I didn't know what to do because I didn't want to worry Jessica, but if Calvin was cheating on her, then she should know. Then again, if it was Tom and he was lying to me, then I could have stirred up Jessica and Calvin's relationship for nothing. I just needed some time to process the situation.

With about one week left until the school season ended and with summer holidays around the corner, Tom and I texted back and forth a bit that week and he wanted to know if we were still on for our summer road trip. I thought about what had happened and decided that I would take his word for it: that he hadn't done anything with Brittany, but I also told Calvin that if he had something to share with Jessica that he should be honest. He sounded like he didn't know what I was talking about either so I decided to leave it alone and focus on making things better with Tom and enjoying our summer together. Still, it was difficult to believe him with Brittany's choice of words and the sequence of events.

We ended up going on the road trip together and initially it was a little quiet as we hadn't seen each other face to face and had only spoken by text and one phone call all week. As we got further away from the college, we started talking more about our vacation plans and things we would like to see. The first night in the hotel, we just lay in bed and talked. There was nothing intimate as I was still not 100% comfortable about the whole Brittany thing. We talked about our relationship and the future and Tom kept reassuring me that I was his future and he was mine. We both fell asleep as it was a long first day on the road and we were planning on getting up early to start driving again.

The next morning he brought me coffee and breakfast which started the day off great. He kissed me and told me how happy he was that we were on this trip together. That started the day great and we hit the road to our next destination. This drive was more relaxed and we seemed to begin to get to our old rhythm back, laughing and just being us. That night we checked into a hotel and went for a nice dinner in the hotel restaurant. Afterwards we went for a dip in the pool around 10 pm. There was nobody in the pool and Tom came up to me, grabbed me and kissed me sensually and said "I miss this so much," to which I smiled and said "me too." He kissed me again and this time it was more passionate. I wanted him so badly in that moment. He climbed out of the pool and reached for my hand to help me out: I wasn't sure where he was taking me. He walked towards the sauna room and opened the door. Nobody was in it. As I followed him in, he turned and kissed me, and picked me up, holding me against the wall. He told me how he wanted me right then and there. He slid off the bottom of my bikini and right there in the sauna he made love to me. For a split second I was worried that someone would walk in on us, but the rest of the time I was in the moment and loved every second of it.

After our amazing moment in the sauna we went back up to the room and lay in bed and enjoyed a couple glasses of wine together. He told me how much he loved me and couldn't see himself being with anyone else. Naturally this made me smile and I returned the feelings. The wine had made me sleepy and I fell asleep in his arms shortly after that.

The next morning we were on the road again and Tom and I were getting along better than we had in a long time. We had the best trip seeing sites that we had both never seen before and making memories with all of our adventures. On the second-to-last day, he wanted to take me on a hike to the top of a mountain. I was always up for a challenge. Although I admittedly wasn't a big fan of heights, I agreed to go. As we approached the highest peak of the mountain, Tom ran ahead to check it out, telling me he wanted to make sure it was safe. He ran ahead and within a minute he was out of my sight. As I kept climbing I came around the last peak, only to see Tom there down on one knee and holding a flower.

I instantly started to tear up. I hadn't been expecting this at all. I knew we were young, but I also knew that he was everything I had ever wanted. As I neared him, he reached out for my hand and said, "Kerry, I know we may seem young in many people's eyes, but I also know that meeting you just over a year ago was the best thing that ever happened to me. You make me want to be a better man and I love you so much. I'm not saying we have to get married in the next year or anything, but I want to spend the rest of my life with you. Will you marry me?"

I started sobbing. "Tom, you have made me realize what love is and I want to spend my life with you. Yes, I will marry you". He put a ring on my finger and stood up and kissed me. I couldn't believe I had just gotten engaged. I was happier than ever and everything seemed perfect.

7

Trouble in Paradise

Our summer trip ended on a high: literally as we were on top of a mountain as well as figuratively as Tom had proposed to me. We had been gone almost a month and decided to come back to campus to work a bit and spend time with friends before school started. We hung out with Jessica and Calvin and they also seemed to be doing well.

When we broke the news to them they were both surprised, but also very happy for us. I naturally asked Jessica to be my maid of honor and amazingly Tom asked Calvin to be in the wedding party. He didn't say best man because Tom told me on the drive home that that spot was being held for his brother. Calvin agreed to be in the wedding party so that was exciting for us that we were all going to be together. We told them it wouldn't likely be until we graduated, which would be in two years, but we had wanted to let them know we wanted them to be part of it.

Another school year started and I was nervous as I had also started to work with clients in a counselling set-up this semester on real personal issues. I felt like I knew enough, but there is added pressure to be competent when you start something new, especially dealing with other people's lives. I also started back at Books & Beans as I needed money to pay for my schooling, and now a wedding in a couple of years.

I hadn't seen Brittany yet and we were already two weeks into the school year. I knew she was in her last year so I still expected to see her around at some point. The following week Tom was having coffee in the shop while I was working one evening and in walked Brittany. She ordered from me and tried to be nice, but I still thought she was fake. Even at some of our sorority functions she was this sweet girl at times, mostly in front of guys, then acted all snobby to most of the other girls when no boys were around. However, I was at work so I tried to be professional and kind. She grabbed her coffee and went and sat down at the table next to Tom. I could smell a faint orange smell as she walked towards his table, similar to the one in the dorm, but I didn't pay much attention to this as I was focusing more on the fact that she was going to sit down with Tom. I couldn't help but watch. I noticed she said 'hi' to him, to which he responded and then looked over at me. He seemed to try and ignore her and then about 5 minutes later as she got up to leave, I noticed she slipped him a piece of paper. He grabbed it and looked at her as if to give it back, but she was already gone. "What did she give him?" I wondered. A love note, her phone number?

I walked over to him to see what it was and he didn't hesitate to show me. I think he wanted to show me that I could trust him. It read 'meet me at the library'. I asked him why she would be asking him that if there was nothing between them, especially since he had a girlfriend, or should I say fiancée. Also, if they hadn't spoken in over two months, why had she approached him as if they had recently talked? I had been with Tom almost the entire summer so I did trust him and we were engaged so I didn't think I had anything to worry about, but I still didn't like the fact that she was once again throwing herself at my Tom. He told me that maybe she wanted to study as they had one class together, but that he wouldn't study with her given the circumstances and out of respect for me. He kissed me and said he was heading back to his dorm room. I had to keep working for a couple of more hours but I was more than a little stressed after what had just transpired.

Shortly after he left, I texted Jessica and asked her to do me a favor: go to the library, but not be seen by Tom. I had to know if he was going to meet Brittany and if there was anything going on. She didn't even hesitate to help me out and agreed to go. Jessica told me later that night that she had gone to the library and was in one of the aisles, innocently looking for a book and had seen Brittany waiting in a study carrel. A couple of minutes later, Tom did show up. They were talking and Brittany seemed to make an advance towards him, but he grabbed her and stopped her. Jessica said she couldn't hear exactly what they were saying but he looked upset that she was trying to come on to him, but also that they somewhat looked like they had talked more than just saying hello in the past. I was happy to hear he didn't welcome her advances, but it did make me wonder why he would have actually met her if there was nothing between them.

When I asked him where he was that night, he did tell me he went to the library and also told me that Brittany tried to come on to him. He said he simply went there to tell her to stop trying to get with him and that he was engaged to me. I took this for what it was and was happy he was honest with me. For the next several months, I rarely saw Brittany, only a few times at the Pool Shark from a distance and although she would look over at Tom, she never came over and talked to him with me there. She seemed to have finally taken the hint, at least from what I could see.

Over the rest of the semester I got to experience working with clients and realized how stressful this type of work was. I knew you were not supposed to take the work home with you or personally, but it was hard when so many people were dealing with big problems in their lives. That being said, I also found it very rewarding to help people and I had the support of my supervisor during my practicum hours. As the end of my third year approached, I was looking forward to another summer off, some extra time with Tom, and maybe even starting to plan our wedding. That summer we did some camping but for the most part we stayed around campus as I wanted to work more hours to help pay for the wedding. Tom also worked at a bar near the campus so that he could contribute to the wedding as well, so we didn't get to see each other as much as the previous summers, but we still managed to get some quality time in here and there.

There were a few times while Tom and I were hanging out that I noticed he was on his phone more than usual. I didn't think much of it, but it started to become more of an issue as he would be on it even when we out at a restaurant together or when we were out with friends. I asked him once who he was talking to or texting all the time and he just told me it was family. One night when Tom was in the shower, I heard his phone beep and so I decided to go see the notification as it was locked. The front of the phone just had a message on it that read "Phone me, I need to talk to you", but it didn't say who it was from. I heard the shower shut off so I rushed back to sit on the couch. Tom was never one to keep secrets but the last couple of months he had been more distant. I just figured it was because we hadn't been spending as much time together. I didn't want to pry but admittedly my curiosity about that text stayed with me.

School was about to start the following week and it was my final year. Calvin, Jessica, Tom, and I decided to go out to the Pool Shark for some drinks before we started classes. We were having a great time, but then I noticed Brittany sitting by herself in the back corner of the bar. What the hell was she doing here? She was supposed to have graduated last year. I looked at Tom to see if he had noticed her, and it didn't seem like he had. Then I saw him look at his phone and glance around the bar. I looked over at Brittany and she was looking his way. Could she have been who was texting him, now and before? Before I knew it, Tom told us that he would be right back. I couldn't help but follow discreetly. He headed toward the washrooms and I saw Brittany head that direction as well. I stayed out of sight, but was near enough to the hallway that I could still hear them.

"I thought I told you to stay away from me?" Tom said firmly. "We can't be doing this anymore. I'm getting married next year and you keep trying to contact me."

"Tom, you know how I feel, so why don't you leave her," replied Brittany.

"That's not going to happen so you need to move on. I'm not warning you again". Then I turned the other direction so he wouldn't notice me as I saw him walk briskly away from the washrooms. I grabbed a couple of drinks from the bar and headed back to the group. I gave Tom his drink and he smiled and thanked me. I asked if everything was okay and he took a drink and said "Yeah, just fine" but in a somewhat dubious tone.

Their conversation made me wonder if all this time he had been lying to me and actually cheating on me. The time I saw Brittany and a guy through the wall, the innocent hellos in the coffee shop, the invitation to the library and now this. I heard him tell her to stop contacting him, but a part of me still wanted to know the truth; had he had sex with her, was he calling or texting her? That didn't seem like Tom at all. Part of me just wanted to believe he wouldn't do that and the fact that I heard him tell her to leave him alone should have been confirmation enough that he wanted to be with me, but I didn't want to have a marriage based on lies. That night as I lay in bed, I texted Tom; "Hey babe, I need to ask you something and I just want you to be honest with me. It's been bothering me all day. I overheard you and Brittany talking at the Pool Shark and you saying you guys can't do this anymore. Also, a few months ago you met her at the library after she left the coffee shop. Is there something I should know?"

It took about ten minutes for him to reply.

"Kerry, there's nothing going on between Brittany and me. I admit she wanted to get together with me, but I told her that I'm happy with you. End of story." I wanted to believe him and I guess that's all I could do given the circumstances, but it just all seemed to connect to him without any proof. I decided that I had to take him at his word. "Ok, I believe you," I texted back. Part of me was still not 100% sure.

The next several weeks were a little stressful as I was back in school for my final year and had a heavy course load, I was still working at the coffee shop, and Tom and I were trying to get past this whole Brittany thing. I continued to focus on my schooling and as things started to settle down, Tom and I started talking about the wedding again as we were planning to do it in the summer after graduation, which was only about seven months away at this point. As I went about my daily and weekly routine, I couldn't help but notice that I had not seen Brittany at the coffee shop or Pool Shark in the past couple of months. Maybe she had finally gotten the message and decided to move on with her life.

We were approaching the midway point of the school year which meant we had just finished some finals for the semester, so to unwind a bit, the four of us decided to go out on the town and celebrate completing some of our classes. We were having an amazing time and while we were waiting for our Uber to pick us up, we noticed a sign posted on a board near the bus stop where we were waiting. The sign read, "Missing girl - Brittany Galloway, age 23" and a picture of her. My stomach went into knots as we had just seen her a couple months previously. I was shocked to see someone who I knew on a missing person poster.

I looked at Tom and he looked like he was trying to show concern, but not overly fazed by seeing the posting. Our Uber arrived and as we all got in, I wondered what had happened to her. I had obviously not liked her and had wanted her to leave Tom alone, but I could never wish anything bad upon anyone, including her. We continued to our next stop which was some pub. The boys were looking to have more drinks as they didn't seem bothered by the Brittany thing, yet I couldn't get it out of my mind, even though I tried to have fun. I asked Tom whether he was worried about her and he just shrugged his shoulders and said "I'm sure she'll show up," and then continued playing darts with Calvin. I guess I just assumed that he would be a little more concerned as we had both interacted with her on several occasions and now she was missing. We continued enjoying the rest of our evening, but I definitely thought about what had happened to Brittany throughout the night.

When Jessica and I got back to our dorm room, I asked her about what she thought about the Brittany situation and she just replied by saying "I'm not overly surprised as she seemed to be kind of a bitch. It's unfortunate though. Maybe someone had a bone to pick with her." When I told her about what I heard at the Pool Shark that night, she said that was kind of a weird conversation, but then added, "You don't really think Tom had something to do with her disappearance, do you?"

"No, but it is strange that she went missing not long after that conversation."

"Tom is a sweetheart Kerry, he wouldn't hurt anyone." Jessica replied.

"I know. I guess it just bothers me not knowing what happened to her and wondering if Tom was actually talking to her."

8

Till Death Do Us Part

The coffee shop I worked in had two televisions, each in a corner of the shop. I often caught myself watching the news while I was waiting for customers at the counter. About a week after we saw the missing- person poster for Brittany, there was a breaking news piece on TV during one of my shifts. The headline at the bottom read, "University grad found dead," then "Brittany Galloway, dead at 23. Suspected homicide." I dropped the coffee mug I was holding and spilled coffee all over the counter. My hands were shaking as I could not believe what I had just seen.

Moments later, Tom walked into the coffee shop and he looked at me behind the counter and could see I was in shock, then turned to the TV and saw the running headline. He came up to me and I asked him if he had heard about it and he replied, "No, I saw it just now. That's so sad." Then he asked me how I was doing. I told him I was in shock and didn't know why someone would do this to her. He asked me if I needed him to do anything for me and I shook my head. I told him maybe we could do something later just to take my mind off what had happened. He offered to take me out for dinner and a movie, to which I agreed. I tried to enjoy the evening with Tom, but I was still shaken up by what had happened to Brittany. "Someone actually killed her," I thought to myself. "Who would do such a thing?"

The following weeks I kept watching the news to see if there were any updates on Brittany's case, hoping to find out more about what had happened to her: more importantly, who was responsible. With all the commotion going on I still had to focus on my schooling as I was only four months away from graduating. Also, our wedding was only five months away and we hadn't done much planning so needless to say there was a bit of stress in my life.

A couple of more weeks flew by and with the Brittany thing somewhat fading into the background and no updates, Tom and I focused on planning for our big day. We hadn't planned a big wedding, but there was still a lot to do as I wanted it to be special. I only planned on this being a one-time event for us.

Tom was helpful in planning, but he basically let me make all the decisions. Anything I asked him to look into for me he was more than willing. It was tough juggling work, school, practicum hours, and planning the wedding, but I think I managed the best that I could. As my last set of finals approached I took a couple weeks off from planning the wedding as I wanted to make sure I finished my exams with top marks so I could finish my degree with honors; I figured this would help with job opportunities after and I also hoped to get into a Masters' program in psychology, which would be very competitive. I had worked very hard the past four years and looked forward to finishing on a high note.

I finally wrote my last exam and we all headed to the Pool Shark for drinks to celebrate the completion of four long years and a lot of drama. While at the bar, something caught my eye. On one of the walls was a bulletin board, where bands or local cash jobs could be posted for free advertising. There was a flyer with Brittany's picture on it promoting a fundraiser in her name. The goal was to raise money for a reward for information regarding finding her killer. In the midst of our celebration, here was another reminder of a tragic event that I had managed to put behind me.

Then something strange happened. While we were sitting having drinks, a girl came up to our table and looked directly at Tom and said, "Weren't you with Brittany the day she went missing?" She seemed to know him.

Tom looked confused and replied that he didn't know what the girl was talking about. "I think you have me mistaken for someone else," he retorted.

"No, she told me she was going to meet you that day because she had something important to tell you."

"I'm sorry to tell you, but I wasn't with that girl that day, or any other day for that matter. I was with my fiancée that day," Tom replied back calmly, but sternly. He then said he was leaving and didn't have to sit there and listen to such nonsense. I followed him out towards the car, but we had to wait for Jessica and Calvin as they had driven with us. While waiting with him I started wondering: how would he have known what day Brittany went missing? It could have just been the way he said it but it was still an odd response, especially if he had nothing to do with it as he had said he hadn't. I kind of pushed the thought away and didn't think much more of it than just his choice of words, but it was more difficult not to remember my past uncertainties about his interactions with her.

Calvin and Jessica came out a few minutes later and we all headed back to the dorms. The next day we slowly started to pack up our stuff as we had about two weeks to move out, plus graduation, and then two weeks after that was our wedding. Needless to say there was a lot going on. Tom and I did some cake tasting on the weekend and finalized some other details of the ceremony and reception. I couldn't wait to see my parents as it had been almost six months since I had seen them last when Tom and I went home for Christmas and we got to spend a bit of time with them.

My dad seemed to like Tom and they bonded over sports and talking about their favorite teams. My mom seemed to like him too, but I could tell she was holding something back. One time on the phone, a couple of months earlier, I had asked her about our Christmas visit and she said she liked him and thought he was nice and sweet, but there was just something about him that she didn't trust, like he wasn't being fully honest. Naturally this worried me a bit because I had shared such feelings and, after all, mother knows best. That being said, aside from her feelings, Tom seemed genuine and always seemed to have my best interests at heart and really cared for me. She said she was excited for me to get married, however she did think I was a bit young; nonetheless she supported me.

As graduation day approached I was excited and nervous because I had busted my ass for this degree, but nervous for the next step in my life. There was a big reception planned following our walk on the stage to accept our degrees. My parents were both in attendance and I could see Tom in the crowd as well as he was sitting with his faculty waiting to go on stage after me. We had a great night partying with our friends, many of whom we would see at our wedding a couple of weeks later. A few days after grad, Tom and I went to look at a few smaller houses because we needed some place to stay once we had to leave campus.

We wanted to find a place before we got married so we could move our stuff and start off being newlyweds in our new place. We couldn't afford a big house to start off, but we had saved enough to make a small down payment and Tom had a steady income with his new business he had started last year. We looked at about six different places, five of which were in town but really expensive, and then one listing that was somewhat out in the woods, fairly secluded but nice and quiet. This listing had a lot of trees surrounding the one area of the lot which went on for quite a bit. I am not sure exactly where the end was, but the realtor mentioned there was a train station about a mile away.

Tom said he liked this secluded house the best and although I was a city girl, I liked the idea of a quiet area and being able to work on my master's with nature around me. We put an offer on the house and two days later it was accepted. We were so happy. We moved all of our stuff into the house two days later and went shopping for some basic furniture. We didn't need a lot to start with, and we had used most of our savings on our down payment, but this was our place to call our own and my life felt like it was finally starting.

The day after we moved in, we met our neighbors and they invited us to a BBQ the next day. They were a nice couple about five years older than us. She was Taylor and her husband was Brad. She was very attractive and although Brad was not exactly a GQ cover kind of guy, he was a successful businessman and seemed quite nice. Taylor stayed home a lot as she was a writer so she spent a lot of her days writing and doing things around the yard. Tom and I went to the BBQ as we wanted to make a good first impression and thought it would be good to get to know them, especially if we needed anything in the future.

For the most part, we hung out in their backyard around the pool as Brad cooked outside. Their house was beautiful and had windows all around the perimeter and lit up at night so it wasn't hard to miss from the road. At one point I was talking to Brad and noticed Tom had gone inside to help Taylor. I could somewhat see them in the kitchen through the window and looked like they were getting along as I heard her even laugh at one point. About ten minutes later they both came out with some more food to go with the steaks Brad was grilling. Tom came up to me and kissed my forehead. "Your wife is quite the accomplished writer," Tom said to Brad. Then Tom looked at Taylor and smiled.

"Yes, she has written some fine books," he responded.

"She seems like quite a catch," Tom said back to him. I'm sure he was just being nice, but it was kind of an odd comment, especially with me sitting right here.

"Thank you. Your fiancée seems great too!" Brad quickly replied as if he could feel that Tom was almost clueless to the fact that I was sitting right there listening to him say that.

Tom replied "Yes, I am a lucky man! We're getting married next week. I know we just met, but we are neighbors now so why don't you guys come. I'm sure we have room for two more." Then Tom looked at me for approval.

"Sure, that would be lovely," I replied. As if I really had the choice to say anything but that in front of them.

"Well, let's eat," Brad let out with relief. We enjoyed our meal and some wine and walked home about two hours later. On the way home, Tom asked if I was alright because I wasn't as talkative as usual. The truth was that I was more than a little annoyed at his comments as he seemed to be flattering Taylor rather than bragging about his fiancée. I mentioned this to him as I wanted to be honest, but didn't want to come across as being jealous or whatever. He simply responded by saying he was just being nice to our new neighbors, to which I replied, "I know". I guess I just had to take it at that. When we got home I was exhausted and went straight to bed.

The following weekend was our wedding and I spent the week writing my vows, picking up my dress, and tying up all the loose ends that a wedding entails. We wanted to have everyone celebrate together so had planned a bachelor/bachelorette party for two days before our wedding. I may have also had an ulterior motive: I didn't want Tom going to see nasty strippers. You hear stories of what happens at those things and although I trusted Tom, I figured it would be better to avoid the situation altogether. He seemed fine with doing the combined party as he said he wanted to celebrate with me, so it all worked out.

The night of the bachelor/bachelorette party, we rented a limo bus and did a huge scavenger hunt all related to a wedding theme. We drank in the bus, played music, and had a blast. Of course the girls' team won the scavenger hunt, which just meant we had to have more shots. Let's just say I'm glad we weren't getting married the next day because a hangover is not a good look for a bride. The pictures we took during the scavenger hunt were definitely something to laugh about.

We both took the next day to recover and made a few calls to confirm our guest list, and that night I made Tom stay at Calvin's and Jessica stayed with me. Maybe it was just superstition, but I didn't want him seeing me in my dress before the wedding. Jess and I talked all night and she asked me if I was nervous or ready for this big step. I told her I was ready, but I would be lying if I said I wasn't nervous. It wasn't just because I was young. A few of the things that happened over the past couple of years with Tom still felt like there were unanswered questions, but I had tried not to read anything into them. I figured I had better get some sleep as I didn't want to have bags under my eyes on my wedding day.

The next morning, Jessica, another friend of mine and I all got our makeup and hair done professionally and then we were picked up by a limo to head to the church. We only had about 70 guests at our wedding which included many friends from school and mostly my family. Tom's mother, who I had never actually met in person, showed up. We had done a video call with her once or twice over the past three years and that had been it. Tom also had a long-time friend, whom I had never met before, show up as well. His name was Jordan. He looked a little rough but was Tom's friend so I welcomed him with open arms. As the girls and I waited in the back room, I could hear the organ playing and I knew that I would soon be walking down the aisle. Both bridesmaids went, then it was my turn. As I stood at the back of the church and looked at

Tom in the distance, I felt a calm come over me as I knew I wanted to spend the rest of my life with him. Nothing would ever change that. As I put one foot in front of the other, I tried not to fall in the crazy heels I had chosen. It also helped that I was holding my dad's arm. I could see Tom smiling at me as we locked eyes.

While walking down the aisle, for a split-second, a girl about my age caught my eye and she had this look on her face as if she was trying to tell me something. Obviously I wasn't about to stop walking, but my eyes drew back to her as she tried to mouth some words to me. It looked like she was saying "Get down or get out," which made no sense to me and I wasn't even sure that's what she was saying. I hoped I didn't have something sticking out of my dress as that would have been embarrassing. My eyes went back to Tom and as I approached him, my dad gave me away and Tom reached for my hand. As we stood there, facing one another, listening to the priest talk, I thought about all the times Tom and I had shared and how happy he had made me feel. Sure there were a few hiccups along the way, but I truly loved him and knew he cared more about me than anything else. I almost got lost in my own thoughts as I suddenly heard the priest ask me to repeat after him. We then both said the vows we had written and Tom's made me tear up because they were so beautiful.

We shared a soft kiss and recessed down the aisle and out of the church.

The reception was beautiful, with elegant decorations around the hall. One thing I had really wanted was a candy bar as I had seen it at a wedding I had been to and thought it would be fun for everyone when I got married. So we definitely had to have one and we also had a chocolate fountain for those who like dipping their candies as well. The table centerpieces were stunning flower arrangements sitting in bowls of water, each with a candle in it. Each table had a bottle of white and red wine on it and we had a set menu with dinner served, rather than buffet style. The food was amazing. Before we let people get too carried away with tinging glasses to make us kiss, we let everyone know that if they wanted Tom and me to kiss, they were to do either a one-minute dance or sing at least one minute of a song of their choice. We thought this would be a fun way to get everyone involved and avoid the annoying constant tinging of glasses. It definitely made for some good laughs as many people gave their best shot at dancing and singing in order to get us to kiss.

After dinner we had the speeches and Jessica, being my maid of honor, said a few words. She went on to tell me how lucky she was to have met me in college and how I was like the sister she had never had. She continued with some of our memories together and wished us a happy marriage. She also had a few words for Tom.

"Tom, we met shortly after I met Kerry and I see how happy you make her and that's all anyone could ask for. My simple request to you is that you make her your priority and love and protect her for the rest of your life…..and if you ever break her heart or hurt her, you'll have to deal with me," she said with a smile and a chuckle. Everyone laughed, but Tom gave a small grimace, as though he wasn't overly impressed by that last comment. He tried covering up, however, by smiling along with the others and being a good sport.

Our MC took the microphone after that, perhaps sensing a bit of awkwardness and said it was time for the first dance and then the father of the bride dance. Tom and I had picked the song "Perfect" by Ed Sheeran and he held me close as we moved slowly together on the dance floor. He whispered in my ear how much he loved me and how lucky he was to be my husband. Everyone was watching us dance as he finished with dipping me and sealing it with a kiss.

It was now time for my dance with my dad. This was emotional for me because my dad and I were always so close while I was growing up and I hadn't seen him as much while I was away at college, but we had managed to talk several times a week. It had been much less that last year and that made me sad, so standing there on my wedding day, holding my dad was, I was overcome with emotion. He told me how beautiful I was and how proud of me he was and I started to cry. As we danced to the song "I loved her first", he also told me that Tom seemed like a great guy and that if I ever needed anything he was always there for me. We finished our dance and then it was time to cut the cake.

Our cake was a three-tiered vanilla cake with a cream filling. It had elegant flower decorations around it and a traditional bride and groom on the top, but we added a little something extra on ours; we had a piece of fondant made to look like a rope in a knot and the bride and groom holding each end, representing "tying the knot." Maybe it was a bit cheesy, but we liked it. After we cut the cake and I shoved a piece in Tom's face, he returned the favor and then kissed me with a face full of cake and vanilla icing. After we cleaned up, it was time to really party. Almost everyone danced throughout the evening and had plenty to drink, but something odd happened while we were dancing.

That girl from the church came up to me later in the evening and said she needed to talk to me. I asked what about and she whispered in my ear, "Be careful," and right after that, Tom showed up, gave that girl a bit of a dirty look, and then pulled me to the dance floor. I asked him if he knew her and he said no and that he thought it was a friend of mine that I had invited. I had never seen her before today though. I thought it was odd for someone to say such a thing and especially on my wedding day, but by now we had quite a bit to drink so I kind of brushed off what she had said and continued to party.

Throughout the night Tom and I walked around talking to people separately and at one point I remember looking around for him and I noticed he was standing near the bar talking with Taylor. They were both having a drink and then walked towards the dance floor. They started dancing together, not a slow song, but nonetheless dancing together. As the song was coming to an end I decided to walk over towards them to see what was going on. As I approached them, a slow song began and I asked Tom to dance. Taylor smiled at both of us, congratulated us on our wedding and went to sit back at her table with Brad.

"So what was that all about?" I asked.

"What was what," Tom said, obviously confused.

"Now you're dancing with our neighbor?" I asked in a bit of a snarky tone. I know it sounded jealous, but I didn't think I would be the only one to find this a bit odd, would I? Maybe it was the alcohol talking.

"What? I was just talking and thanked her for coming. She asked to dance and it's not like we were holding each other so I don't see the big deal, sweetie. Have a drink and loosen up." Tom replied.

"I'm sorry, I didn't mean to read into it." I was sorry, but still thought it was a bit strange, but didn't let it ruin my night. Everyone continued to party and not too many people left early.

That night Tom had booked us the penthouse suite in the hotel where the reception was held so that when we were done partying we could just go upstairs and have our own little private party. It was getting quite late, but I wanted to consummate our new marriage with some romance so I suggested we go up to our room. Naturally enough, Tom didn't object. We had sex three times: in the shower, on the sofa, and finally in bed. What a perfect night for an amazing day.

Before we went to sleep, I gave Tom my wedding present to him. The first part was a bracelet as I knew he liked wearing them, but this one had our wedding date engraved on the inside of it. The other part of my present was a gold letter 'K' that he could put on his key chain so that he could take me with him everywhere. He loved both gifts and put the 'K' on his keychain immediately and put on the bracelet. The next morning we had room service and enjoyed breakfast as Mr. and Mrs. Gipoli and discussed our honeymoon to the Bahamas in a week. This was the first day of the rest of our lives together.

9

The Honeymoon

t was a couple of days before our flight was going to leave for the Bahamas. We were both so excited, but I think I was a little more than Tom. I had never travelled outside of the U.S. before and after he showed me where we were going, it was easy to be excited. Tom had surprised me with the destination the day after our wedding. I jumped up and down and screamed, which was followed by asking him how he could afford it to which he just told me not to worry about it, it was his gift to me.

We had talked about our honeymoon over the past year and he knew the Bahamas, specifically the Atlantis Paradise Island, was the one place I was dying to stay at. I had heard stories of other people visiting this resort and a lot of celebrities stayed there and I knew this was where I wanted our honeymoon, but I never would have imagined that we could afford it. I tried to ask Tom a couple of other times how much it cost because being married, I naturally thought we should discuss finances, but he continued to tell me not to worry and that he wanted this honeymoon to be perfect and to make me happy. I mean how could I argue with that, so I finally stopped asking.

With only a couple of days until we left, I still needed to get a few things: sandals were at the top of my list, but I also needed a sarong and a new pair of sunglasses. I asked Jessica to come with me for a shopping day as Tom wasn't really into shopping that much. Plus he had told me he wanted to get a few things done around the yard before we left and was also going to go for a run. Living out in the country meant there was a lot of open road to jog on as our neighbors Taylor and Brad were about 500 yards away. Jessica arrived and gave a honk at me to come out. Tom stopped the lawnmower as he saw Jessica pull up and they exchanged hellos, then I gave him a kiss goodbye and told him I would be back in a couple of hours. He asked me to pick him up a pair of sandals as well. Jessica and I had a nice chat on the way to the mall. We discussed my being married and our honeymoon coming up, and she told me how she and Calvin were moving in together as well, which I was very happy to hear. We had a great time together and even went for lunch at this nice outdoor restaurant in town. We drove down our long country road and as we approached Taylor and Brad's house, in the distance I saw Tom standing at the end of their driveway talking to Taylor. Tom was wearing shorts and had no shirt on as he sometimes jogged without one. I told Jessica to slow down to see what they were doing. It looked like innocent chit chat and then she laughed and touched his shoulder. As we got closer I honked the horn and we rolled the windows down.

"Hey guys," I said casually as if I didn't mind her touching my husband's shirtless body.

"Hey hun. I'm just out for my run and saw Taylor in the yard," he said. "Did you two have fun shopping?"

"We did," I said, but not overly enthused. "I got the sandals you asked me to pick up."

"You're amazing, thanks! See you at home after my run."

"Sure thing," I said, straining hard to smile.

As Jessica continued to drive toward our driveway, I looked in the mirror to see if Tom was staying to talk to Taylor or leave to continue his jog. It took him about 30 seconds, but he put his headphones back on and continued his jog.

Jessica gave me a bit of a look and I said "What?" She said "Tom loves you, but I would keep an eye on her."

The next night we asked Taylor and Brad over for a drink to return the favor for the BBQ the previous week, but we also wanted to ask them to keep an eye on the house while we were gone. They said they were more than happy to help us out. We shared a few drinks while we sat around our fire pit talking about work, our honeymoon, and relationships. They told us that they had been married for about five years and shared some advice on a successful marriage, but also admitted that it wasn't always rosy, that it took work. They said they were thinking about having kids soon, but were also enjoying the freedom of travelling whenever they wanted and spending time together. Well those were Brad's words. Taylor seemed to partially agree but added, "You should make sure to keep things interesting so you don't get bored with one another." Maybe I read into this, but I kind of got the impression she was referring to herself, possibly being a little bored with her hubby. Maybe Jess was right: maybe I had better keep an eye on her.

Shortly after that I mentioned to Tom that we had to get up quite early for our flight so we better finish packing and get to bed. We gave them a key to our place and thanked them again as they walked back to their house.

As we brought the empty glasses and bottles into the house, I asked Tom if he had heard what Taylor had said about being bored with your partner. He said he had, but that she was probably just saying we should keep things spontaneous and adventurous. I told Tom I thought she was somehow implying she was bored with Brad and maybe she was looking at him for some excitement. Tom pulled me close to him and chuckled, "Oh you think so hey? Well I think we have plenty of adventure and I only want you." Then he kissed me, picked me up and carried me to the living room where we made love. Now it was definitely getting late so we quickly packed the rest of our things so we would be ready for the morning.

Morning came and I was so tired from our late night, but I was equally excited to be heading to the Bahamas. We arrived at the airport about two hours before our flight and checked our bags. After that, we were both hungry as we hadn't really had time for breakfast since we had slept in as long as we could. We each grabbed a coffee and some food at a little coffee shop in the airport and talked about what we wanted to do when we arrived at the resort. Tom mentioned swimming with the dolphins, which I was up for, but a little nervous at the same time. I was looking forward to being pampered with massages and pedicures, but told Tom I was up for anything.

Our flight was on time. We boarded the plane and got settled in our seats. I was a little nervous as I had never flown before, much less a long flight overseas like this. Tom thought it would be a good idea for us to get a glass of wine, or in his case rum. Even though it was only 10 a.m. by now, he thought it was a good way to settle my nerves and celebrate the start of our honeymoon. Normally I would have said no, but given the circumstances I agreed to have one, but we had to wait until we got in the air. The taking off part was what I was scared of so that didn't help. Tom held my hand as the plane lifted off the ground smoothly; I was still a bit nervous. The flight attendant walked by and I caught her eye and said to her, "Time for that drink." She smiled and said she would be right back with them.

About an hour into the flight Tom leaned over and whispered into my ear.

"Want to be part of the mile-high club?" I had no idea what that meant so he proceeded to tell me.

"No, we can't do that here" I said to him, as if I was shocked he would even ask.

"Babe, it's our honeymoon, let's make memories we'll never forget. You go to the bathroom and I'll come a few minutes later and say I am checking on my wife."

It's not that I didn't want to have fun, I was just nervous about getting caught, but this would take my mind off being nervous about the flight. "Ok, let's do it."

I walked back towards the washroom and even put on a face like I wasn't feeling that well. The flight attendant at the back noticed and asked if I was okay. I said I just had a queasy stomach as it was my first time flying. She said she would bring me a glass of ginger ale. I sat in the tiny airplane restroom, waiting for Tom. A couple of minutes later, I heard a knock.

"Hello" I said expectantly.

"It's Tom. How're you feeling?" He had concern in his voice, as if to sell the fact I was sick.

"Come in," I replied, trying to sound ill.

I opened the door so he could squeeze in. It was tight with both of us in there and not quite sure how we were going to do this, but admittedly I was excited and nervous at the same time. Tom told me that sitting on him would be the easiest way due to the lack of room. He grabbed my cheeks, started kissing me, then slid my pants down and I climbed on top of him. I had to bite my lip so I didn't make any noise, but the spontaneity and moment were amazing. I don't know if it was the rush of being on a plane with people sitting not two feet from the door, but we both enjoyed it very much. We couldn't be too long as it would be suspicious so we got dressed and Tom left first and I heard him ask the rear attendant if she had any Advil, just to make it seem more real that I was actually sick. About a minute later I went back to our seats where Tom was waiting. As I sat down we both looked at each other, grinned and started giggling.

The rest of the flight was smooth with barely any turbulence. We had lunch on the plane, watched a couple of movies, and I was able to sleep for about an hour or so. When I awoke, we were preparing to land so I was once again nervous. I grabbed Tom's hand and then we landed with only a couple of bumps so it wasn't that bad.

We grabbed our bags from the carousel and, as we walked out to get our shuttle, we could feel the hot sun on our faces. Finally we were here. As our shuttle drove to the hotel I looked out the window, taking everything in. It was beautiful with palm trees everywhere. As we pulled up to our hotel, my mouth fell slightly open in awe of the size and beauty of the hotel. I gave Tom a big kiss as the bus stopped and told him how grateful I was that he had brought me here. We checked into the hotel and a guy with a golf cart took us to our room.

Tom insisted he carry me into the room. It was tradition so I didn't mind. As we walked in, it was breathtaking. A large suite with Jacuzzi tub in the living room, large windows looking out at the ocean and a living room with big couches and beautiful decor. The bedroom was almost bigger than ours at home. There was a basket of fruit and a bottle of champagne with rose petals around it for us: it must have been a honeymoon special or something like that.

I asked Tom what he wanted to do first and he said it was up to me. I told him I would like to walk around the resort to see all the amenities now and then maybe hit the beach a bit later. We put away some of our clothes, changed into more-appropriate beach wear than what we had worn on the plane, and headed out for a walk.

The resort was massive so we only saw about half of it after an hour of walking and decided that we would save the rest of it for another day. We headed to the beach to check out the beautiful white sand and we weren't disappointed. The water looked like something out of a movie and I had to put my feet in. As I stood there in the ocean with the water rushing up to my ankles, Tom came up behind me and put his arms around me.

"Well, do you like it here? Is it all you dreamed it would be?"

"All that and more. I love it!" I replied. "I love you."

"I love you too."

We went for a walk down the beach and back which took us over an hour. It was so beautiful hearing the sound of the waves rushing in to shore and feeling the water hit our feet. We talked to some people along the way; some tourists, some locals working on the beach. It was almost 6:00 and we had dinner reservations for 7:30 so we decided to head back to our room to get changed. We were somewhat tired from walking so we had a golf cart come pick us up and take us to the restaurant. The theme for the restaurant was Greek and it was all decorated accordingly. We were seated near the window so we could still see the ocean as we ate, which made it even more romantic. The menu items were things I would never normally eat, or afford for that matter, but it was all-inclusive with a meal plan package Tom had set up for us. We could order anything on the menu and it was all covered, drinks too.

Our server was so nice and had such a vibrant spirit. We told her it was our honeymoon so I think she wanted to make it extra special. She asked where we were from and told us what a beautiful a couple we were. The drinks we ordered were amazing and the food not only looked decadent, but tasted even better. Tom and I talked about our house and what we planned to do with the yard. We also talked about the neighbors, to which he added how nice he thought Taylor was. I agreed, but added that she seemed to me to be a little too flirty. He didn't seem to think she was, rather he just said she was really nice. After we had dessert, we discussed what we wanted to do the next day: maybe horseback riding or a tour of some sort. We decided we would go in the morning to the little booth by the reception where they had all the tours and pricing listed. After dinner we walked back to our room to work off some of the amazing dinner we had just had and

Tom asked me to go into the bedroom as he had a surprise for me. It was the first night here of our honeymoon so I imagined it was something special.

About 15 minutes passed when he asked me to come out of the room. As I came out, there were candles everywhere around the room and the Jacuzzi was filled with water and bubbles and rose petals on top. I also noticed an ice bucket with a bottle of champagne in it near the window. It was beautiful!

He asked me if I wanted to join him in a bath, as if I would say no to an offer like that! He had soft music playing on the living room stereo. We sat in the hot tub, sipping champagne as he rubbed my feet. This went on for about fifteen minutes at which point he reached for my glass, put it on the ledge and pulled me close to him. He started kissing me as we sat close together in the hot tub. He pulled me closer, on top of his lap and I could feel him go inside me. We must have kissed and made love for twenty minutes right there in the Jacuzzi.

Tom stood up, picked me up, got out, and carried me to the bedroom. He was such a fantastic lover, always wanting to please me. He continued to kiss me all over as my body quivered for him, then we made love again and fell asleep in each other's arms.

The next morning after breakfast we headed to the tour booth to see what we wanted to do. After looking at all the options, we decided on a few things for the week. First we were going to do a dolphin swim that day and then a catamaran the following day with dinner on the boat. Another day we planned to do some deep-sea fishing, as we both wanted to try catching something really big. The rest of the time we planned to sit on the beach or by the pool, relax and drink.

I was excited about the dolphin swim, but I was a little apprehensive about getting into the water with a mammal that large. We headed to the aquarium center around 10:30 in the morning and listened to a guide who went over the rules we were to follow. Then we were sized with life jackets and a group of us walked over to where the dolphins were and stood on a ledge in the pool area. Seeing them swimming so close to us made me even more excited and more nervous. One guide used a whistle and her hand gestures to make the dolphin swim right up to our feet and then poke its head out of the water. It was beautiful and I even got to rub my hand on its back.

Then it was time to do the ride with the dolphin. One at a time, a participant would go to the middle of the pool. A dolphin would swim around, the participant would grab onto its flippers, and it would drag the person along for about 20 yards in the water. I was nervous as I wasn't a very good swimmer and thought the dolphin might try to go under water or something. Tom offered to go first so

I could see that it wasn't scary. He was smiling the whole time and looked like he had fun. Then it was my turn. I swam slowly out to the middle where I waited for my ride. Suddenly, with a whistle, I saw a fin coming straight towards me, circle around me, and its flippers were out of the water so I grabbed on and off we went.

I was a little scared but I was also laughing as there was water spraying everywhere and I made it all the way across the pool. What a blast! As I swam back over to the edge where everyone was waiting, Tom told me how proud he was of me and gave me a kiss. That was definitely an experience I would never forget.

Once we got changed from the aquarium, we thought we would go grab a drink and sit on the beach for a while and enjoy the sun. There was barely a cloud in the sky and I could feel the sun beating on me. Our beach was a mile long with white sand and not overly busy, which was also nice. After about an hour had passed, a local guy walked up to us and asked if we wanted to get hemp tattoos. I've always thought about getting a tattoo, but never really could commit to one thing being on my body permanently. This was a good way to see if I would like it for the next week anyway, so I decided to get a butterfly on my foot. Turns out Tom liked it a lot on me as well. We asked the guy to take a picture of us on the beach and make sure he got the butterfly in the picture as well so I could remember it.

After a couple of hours in the sun, we headed back to take a shower to get rid of all the sweat and sand and then go out for dinner. While I was showering, Tom surprised me by joining me. He wrapped his arms around me from behind and kissed my neck. I turned around, kissing him passionately as he picked me up. I wrapped my legs around his waist and he leaned me up against the wall of the shower, making love to me with the water cascading down over both of us. That was definitely a pleasant surprise.

After our little rendezvous we got ready for dinner and headed to a different themed restaurant. Tonight would be Italian. Dinner was amazing yet again, but we both ate so much that we were quite tired, plus we had our catamaran trip the next morning so we figured we would just relax in our room, watch a bit of television, and hit the sack early.

The next morning we went for a quick buffet breakfast before we had to catch our bus to the catamaran. As we arrived we noticed there were about twelve other people going on the catamaran with us. I had been hoping for fewer, but it wasn't that big a deal

I just love being on boats, feeling the sway of the waves, the light breeze and the sun beating down on you. As we boarded and waited to depart, we chatted with a couple of the other tourists. One couple we chatted with were from the U.S. and were really nice. They were around our age, maybe a few years older. They were there on vacation together and had been married for just two years. His name was Paul and his wife was Rachel. We chatted for quite some time, even as the boat pulled away from the dock and headed out for the excursion. This was a full-day trip so we would be eating lunch and dinner there, coming back to our resort just after sunset. The four of us had some drinks together as we stood around the edge of the boat looking for dolphins or whales. Seeing a whale would be a dream come true. Being near something that large and beautiful in person is not something everyone gets to experience.

Before we knew it, lunch was being served so we grabbed a bit and lay down on the front of the boat to eat. They provided a spread of salads, sandwiches, and fruit, and of course more drinks. It was actually pretty tasty. After lunch they stopped in a calm area where we could go snorkeling. They said there were hundreds of different fish and even some turtles if we were lucky. Still a little unsure about getting into deep water with the unknown beneath me, I wasn't about to pass up this opportunity. Tom and I both suited up and jumped in and Paul and Rachel came as well. We were all kind of swimming near each other as our guide had instructed us to stay near him as he swam towards a highly-populated area for fish for us so it was for our safety as well that we all stay together.

About twenty minutes had passed by and I noticed Tom wasn't as close to me as he had been before: I could see him under water, about thirty feet from me. I began to get a little nervous because the next closest person to me was about fifteen feet away, but I didn't want to miss out on any fish so I put my head back in the water, but tried to move towards the group. Another five to ten minutes went by and I must have been focused so much on the fish that I hadn't noticed there was nobody near me. I popped my head up and noticed the nearest person to me was at least thirty feet away.

As I went to dump the water out of my snorkel mask and put it back on, I turned and noticed something very big about two feet from me. Its head came out of the water and I screamed. I started kicking and yelling for help: I was in complete panic. It seemed like forever until someone came and grabbed my arms from behind me and said it was okay. I was crying at this point, but thankful someone was there. It was Paul. He had swum over to help me. I gave him a hug out of relief for feeling saved. He helped calm me down, and also somewhat smiled as he told me it was just a turtle. I felt bad for freaking out, but the feeling of being alone in the deep water and something big coming towards you is not the best feeling to have in the ocean. Paul told me to look under water as he didn't want me to miss seeing it before it swam away. I quickly gathered myself and put my mask on to take a peak. It was one of the coolest things I ever saw. It must have been about 5 feet long by 3 feet wide. As I popped my head back up, I saw Tom finally arrive. He asked if I was okay and I told him Paul had helped calm me down.

"It was just a turtle, Tom. I drifted away from the group and then I saw this big thing coming toward me and panicked."

Tom laughed and thought it was a little silly, but did say in a somewhat sarcastic voice, "Well I'm glad Paul was there to help you."

I told him it wasn't funny in the moment.

We climbed back onto the boat and lay in the sun while the boat gently moved up and down over the waves as it continued on our tour. I must have been tired from the snorkeling as I was very relaxed and fell asleep for about thirty minutes. I woke up with Tom putting an ice cube on my chest and felt it slowly melting on me. He told me they were serving dinner soon.

I was quite surprised with the quality of food on the catamaran. They had chicken skewers, corn, salad, and potatoes, and even dessert for us. Paul and Rachel sat alone while we were laying in the sun, likely because of what happened in the water and Tom's comment, but I invited them to sit with us while we ate as I thought they were nice. We enjoyed dinner and drinks on the back of the boat and found a comfy spot to sit as we were only an hour from sunset.

The tour guide provided blankets for everyone as he noted that the wind picks up as the sun goes down. Tom and I sat there huddled together under a blanket as the sun set. It was one of the most beautiful things I had ever seen. As we got off the catamaran we said good-bye to Paul and Rachel and I asked where they were staying. It turned out they were staying at the same resort as us so I mentioned getting together for dinner the next night and grabbing drinks after. They seemed to like the idea and suggested meeting in the lobby at 7:00.

"Sounds good. See you guys tomorrow night," I said, waving goodbye to both of them. As we walked back to our hotel room Tom didn't seem overly thrilled about meeting them for dinner and when I asked him about it, he sarcastically said, "You just want to have dinner with your knight in shining armor."

"Oh please," I muttered back, "They're a nice couple."

"Whatever," he replied.

We stayed in our room and watched a bit of television until my eyes got heavy and I fell asleep.

The next day we did a beach and pool day, just hanging out enjoying the sun and having drinks. It was nice to just relax as the previous couple of days had been kind of busy. I listened to music and read a little. Periodically I would go for a dip in the pool or ocean, with Tom sometimes joining me and other times staying in his chair. I noticed he had several drinks throughout the day and he was talking a little less clear than usual. When I mentioned he should slow down he told me not to worry about him. I had never seen him like that before. I suggested we head back to the room to get ready for dinner and he said he would meet me there in a bit. I didn't want to start an argument so I just went to the room to get ready.

About thirty minutes had passed, as I got out of the shower and was getting dressed, when Tom finally came into the room. I asked him where he had been and he said he just went for a walk. He apologized for being short with me and said he thought he had just had too much sun, but didn't mention all the drinks he had. I just told him it was fine as I felt it would smooth out the situation rather than starting an argument about his drinking.

We headed to the lobby to meet Paul and Rachel and then walked to dinner together. At dinner we chatted about our tours so far and they told us how they had gone deep-sea fishing and caught a large marlin. We said that we were planning to do that in a couple of days and hearing about their success made us even more excited. We actually had a great dinner and Tom even seemed to be fairly talkative with Paul so maybe the snorkeling incident was behind him. Even so, he did continue to knock back drinks at dinner. After dinner there was a band playing music near the lobby and they even had a dance floor. We all thought it would be fun to grab a drink and watch the band, maybe even dance a little. I enjoy dancing, but Tom isn't a dancer at all, except that time at our wedding. While Paul grabbed drinks for everyone, we found a table. The band was playing so many classics that I wanted to dance, but Tom had no interest. Rachel told Paul to dance with me, obviously knowing it was completely innocent. Paul looked at Tom as if to ask for permission, to which Tom just lifted his chin and gave a slight smile. It was a fast song so it's not like we were holding each other close, but what happened next shocked everyone.

At one point Paul twirled me around and then dipped me, holding me in that position for a second. Truthfully I thought it was innocent, but Tom stormed up towards us and firmly said "Get your hands off her," pushing Paul's hands away from me as he attempted to pull me up from leaning back. I fell in the process.

"What the hell, man!" Paul answered back, confused.

"Why don't you go back to your wife," Tom spit out.

"What's your deal? We were just dancing."

"Yeah, just like you swam to her rescue in the water too, hey?!"

Tom reached for my hand, helped me up and announced that we were going back to our room. I looked at Paul and mouthed the words "I'm sorry" and then at Rachel with the same gesture. Tom was walking quite fast and pulling me along. I asked him to slow down a couple times, but he continued with his pace. When we got into the room, he slammed the door behind us. I was shocked by his actions and asked what his problem was. He said he didn't want some guy putting his hands all over me and that it was the second time in two days that Paul had been all touchy feely. I knew Tom was a bit intoxicated so it may have heightened his emotions, but I also had never seen this jealous side of him before and it worried me. However, I didn't want it to ruin our honeymoon so I tried to talk to him to calm him down.

"Tom, Paul didn't mean anything by what he did and as for the snorkeling incident, I was screaming and scared, and he was the nearest to me. You would have done the same if you heard a girl screaming, wouldn't you?"

"I guess so," he replied solemnly.

"Please don't let this ruin our honeymoon, ok?

"Sorry, I just don't want to lose you," he replied.

"Lose me? We just got married, you won't lose me, but you have to trust me."

"I'm sorry," he answered back.

"I'm going to shower and we can talk more when I get out."

I took a shower to decompress over the situation that had happened and when I got out, Tom was fast asleep. Obviously he had drunk too much, but it was still unsettling to see how he had behaved. I hoped that this had just been a one-time incident.

The next morning, Tom was up early and had gone out to pick up some flowers for me. He had put a little note with the flowers that read: "I'm sorry for my behavior last night and it won't happen again. I love you!"

It was a nice way to wake up. He said he had just had too much to drink and got a little jealous, but he said that he did trust me. Although I thought his actions were over the top, I forgave him because he seemed genuine and it was the first time I had seen him act that way. One silver lining about having something like that happen was the make-up sex. He tried giving me sweet little kisses and I couldn't resist and we made love before going to breakfast.

We didn't see Paul or Rachel at the buffet, nor did we see them by the pool in the morning. That afternoon we went for a walk to a market with little shops as Tom wanted to buy me a little something to make up for his behavior the night before. We saw a lot of interesting items, things we would never find back home, one of which was a special bag that I just had to get. Tom offered to buy it for me as a souvenir, or as I figured, an "I'm sorry" gift. Our shopping took most of the afternoon and we made it back to the hotel around dinner time, except we just went to the buffet. While at the buffet I noticed Paul and Rachel and I looked at Tom to see what his reaction would be. They were sitting about 25 feet from us and hadn't seen us yet. Tom said he would be right back and as I was about to tell him not to go over there, he reassured me it wasn't going to be an issue.

I sat there wondering what he was going to do: I admit that I was a bit uneasy. He walked up to their table and I could see Rachel looked a bit nervous and then looking over at me. She got up and came over to see me. She told me that Paul had been a little shaken up by Tom's behavior and even though I agreed, I tried to downplay it to his being a little inebriated combined with silly petty jealousy. As we both watched the guys talking, Tom extended his hand to Paul as a gesture to what I would assume was an apology. There was a slight delay, but Paul reached out and shook Tom's hand and Tom looked back at Rachel and me with a smile. He then patted Paul's shoulder, but the look on Paul's face did nothing to convince me Tom had genuinely apologized.

Tom returned to our table and I asked him what had happened. He told me that he had apologized for his actions and told Paul he hadn't meant to be so aggressive.

He said Paul told him not to worry and that it was all water under the bridge. Rachel left right then and headed back to Paul. We finished dinner and Tom suggested we go for a walk on the beach but he wanted to stop by the room before we went. He came out of our room with a blanket and a flashlight. I wasn't sure we should be walking on the beach at night, but I felt safe with Tom and the moonlight was bright.

We had been walking for several minutes down the beach and suddenly Tom stopped, pulled me close to him, kissed me, then whispered in my ear, "I want to make love to you right here, right now." I wasn't one for being risqué in public, but it was our honeymoon and the idea of doing it on the beach was somewhat exciting. He laid the blanket down and then laid me down gently on it. It made it easier that I was wearing a dress as I didn't have to take off any clothes. I was thinking a bit about getting caught, but the more he kissed me and started to make love to me, I forgot about everything else. The moonlight on our faces, the sweet taste of his lips from the drink he had had with dinner, and the sand under the blanket that was still a bit warm from earlier in the day. About fifteen minutes went by and as we lay there, we heard voices in the distance so we figured we had better leave in case there was some law against being on the beach at night. We headed back to our room to have a dip in the hot tub and relax. Tomorrow we were going deep sea fishing and I couldn't wait.

The next morning we made it to the buffet for breakfast and there was no sign of Paul or Rachel. It could have just been the time we showed up or maybe they were avoiding us. We didn't have time to wait for them as we needed to get to the marina for 9:00 for a big day of fishing. Tom was very excited as neither he nor I had ever done this before. The boat took us about 30 minutes out from shore and then we got our rods set up. I didn't realize the boat moved while we tried to catch fish, but I guess it was how they did it. About an hour went by and not even a bite and I think Tom was starting to get a little impatient. The tour guide, named Pedro, told him to be patient, but sitting around hoping to catch a massive marlin and not even getting a nibble for over an hour does feel like a waste of time and money for some.

I enjoyed the boat ride, but I also did want to catch something. Another hour passed by and nothing and Tom was getting restless. I saw him go to one end of the boat and talk to one of the tour guides. He looked frustrated. Just as Tom was heading back toward me, the bell on his rod went off; he had caught something. Now all he had to do was reel it in, but I had heard this was no easy task. Tom, with the help of the guide, reeled for almost fifteen minutes trying to pull whatever it was in. It was finally at the boat and I stood up to take a peak over the edge. I took a quick picture of the marlin before they lifted it up. It was enormous and I was amazed Tom had actually caught that. He had such a big smile on his face.

Just as they were trying to use the large net to help lift it into the boat with the cable, the line snapped and the marlin splashed back into the water. Tom's face quickly switched to one of shock and then grabbed Pedro by the vest and shoved him up against the edge of the boat. "What did you do?" he yelled at him, "You lost my prize fish!"

"I'm sorry sir, the line snapped, it was not my fault," the poor guy stuttered. Then Tom looked at me and I think he realized in that moment that his anger was showing once again. He released his hold on Pedro and apologized. "We were so close," he said sadly.

I tried to comfort him by saying we could keep trying, but he was not in the mood to hear that. He just replied with "Yeah, sure". Pedro and the other tour guide got new lines set up so Tom could continue fishing for the two hours left on the tour, but we never got a single bite after that.

"Now nobody will believe I actually caught a marlin," Tom said with disappointment.

"Actually, I snapped this when it was by the boat," I told Tom.

His face lit up again as he was so happy to have proof of his catch. He kissed me and thanked me and said even though we didn't get to bring it into the boat, at least we would have a picture of it. When we got back to the marina we were both starving and decided to do our last theme restaurant for the week and went to the French cuisine restaurant. We changed into different clothes as we smelled like the sea and there was a dress code at this restaurant. Upon arriving, we could see that the restaurant looked gorgeous. It was beautifully decorated and we were lucky to get right in as we hadn't made the usual required reservation. While we were having our wine and appetizers, I looked over and noticed Rachel and Paul across the room. I also saw Tom look towards their table and Paul somewhat reluctantly look back. I told Tom I was going to the washroom and to order my entrée for me.

While in the washroom, Rachel came in to see me. I was happy to see her as we hadn't seen them in a couple of days. I asked what they had been up to and she seemed stressed. She told me they had gone on a tour but that they were also keeping their distance from us. I asked why and she said she would tell me, but that I was not to say anything to Tom. Confused, I agreed. "When Tom came to our table the other day, he apologized for being so aggressive to Paul."

"That's what I heard too. That's great," I replied.

"But then Tom told Paul to keep his hands to himself and mind his own business or there would be trouble."

"What?" I said in disbelief.

"I like you, Kerry and I say this for your sake, please be careful."

"Thanks Rachel, but Tom would never hurt me."

"I'm just saying. I've seen guys like him before. Well I had better get back to my table. Hopefully we can email each other and see you once more before we leave in three days. We likely won't hang out with you guys again before we go, but Kerry, please take care of yourself."

"I will, and it was nice getting to know you guys." With that I gave her a hug and left the washroom.

As I sat down, Tom mentioned that he had ordered for us. While we waited for our food I couldn't help but think about Rachel's words. What was I missing? And why was that girl at the wedding telling me similar things. I knew Tom and he wasn't a bad guy, was he? Was he fooling me? I was starting to have doubts. Tom started talking about what we were going to do for the last couple of days, which took my mind off my negative thoughts.

"Maybe horseback riding?" I suggested. "We also haven't really spent much time on the beach so maybe a day of just relaxing?"

"Both sound good," he replied enthusiastically.

Our dinner came shortly after that and we ate in silence. Afterwards, we headed back to the room. Tom asked if I wanted to go in the Jacuzzi, but I told him I wasn't feeling up to it and that I was just tired. In actuality it was mainly because of the whole Rachel incident.

The next day we went horseback riding in the morning before it got too hot. I had never been on a horse before and it took a little getting used to, but it was a pretty cool feeling to be riding such a big animal. Tom enjoyed himself too, but his horse wouldn't cooperate at times and seemed to want to trot when he didn't want it to which made for a bumpy ride. I thought it was quite funny. He even got a good laugh out of it, that is after arguing with his horse about which direction to go. We stopped for a picnic as part of the tour and then in the afternoon we just cooled off at the pool. That night there was a show at our resort so we both decided to go. While sitting among 200 hundred people watching, I happened to look back to my right and noticed Rachel and Paul sitting in the crowd several rows over and back. She saw me as well and we gave a little wave to one another, but they never came over to talk to us. The show was actually pretty good and Tom seemed to enjoy it as well.

After the show we headed back to the room. Tom and I had had a great day together and I wanted to have a romantic night with him since we were getting close to the end of our trip. I knew that what Rachel had told me was more than a bit concerning, but it was our honeymoon after all and he was so good to me and hadn't shown me anything to be concerned about, except for that night when he was drunk and pushed Paul, but that was one incident and not directed toward me.

So I pulled out some special lingerie I had bought before we left. I hadn't worn it yet because the times we were intimate here had been somewhat impromptu, which hadn't given me the opportunity to change. I asked him to wait in the living room while I changed. He didn't object. When I came out in my lingerie, his eyes lit up like a kid in a candy store. I must admit, I looked pretty sexy. I slowly walked around the couch and moved my body in the sexiest way I could in front of him. Then I climbed onto his lap and we started kissing. From there it was intense passion, stripping of clothes and making love on the couch…then the floor…and finally the bedroom. As we lay there afterwards, I told him I loved him and that he could tell me anything, any secrets he had he could share with me, hoping he would open up. He shrugged it off like there was nothing to tell, then told me he loved me and went to sleep.

The next day was our last full day so we decided to spend most of it at the beach and pool. The sun was shining and there was barely a cloud in the sky. We were able to get a palapa so we didn't get too much sun. We had a few drinks, listened to music, even napped. We also went for a last walk down the beautiful sandy beach. As we started walking back to our palapa Tom stopped me, looked at me and told me how lucky he was that I was his wife and that he would always be there for me. This made me cry as I thought about all the things he had done for me and how amazing this honeymoon was that he had planned for us. I thanked him for taking me to the resort of my dreams and told him I couldn't wait to start our lives together when we got home.

We got back to the palapa, grabbed our things and headed to the room to get ready for our last dinner at the buffet. While we were eating Paul and Rachel saw us at the buffet and came over to our table. Paul spoke up and said to Tom, "I know that you don't want to see us, but we just wanted to say good-bye to Kerry." Paul gave me a hug and then Rachel. I looked at Tom, who had this look like he was fine with them saying good-bye but not overly thrilled with seeing them. Then Rachel faced Tom and said "You better treat her right," to which Tom smiled at her and replied "Of course" and then added "You guys take care" in a somewhat cold, yet sincere, way. They walked away and we sat down and finished our meal. I could tell Tom was a little upset by their appearance at our table but trying to keep his composure.

We went back to our room to relax for our final night. It was getting late when Tom mentioned he had to run out to get a couple of things in the lobby and was also going to do an early checkout so we didn't have to in the morning. I said I would start packing.

About 90 minutes passed and I thought it was odd that he wasn't back yet. I know checkouts can take some time but not that long and certainly not at night. I called the lobby to see if they had seen Tom and asked if we had been checked out yet and they said nobody had been to the lobby checkout counter in over an hour and that we had not been checked out. Now I was starting to get concerned. Where was Tom? After another ten minutes of waiting, I figured I should probably walk around the resort and look for him. Five minutes later the door opened and there he was.

"Where were you? I was getting worried." He was sweating.

Tom told me that he had gone to the little shops to pick up some last-minute souvenirs and some locals had started following him and he had gotten edgy and run away. He had gotten lost around the resort and had made his way back. I said we should contact hotel security, but he insisted we not do that as he didn't want to make a big deal out of it. He said that he was fine and anyway, we were leaving tomorrow. His story sounded plausible, plus he was holding a bag with some souvenirs and told me to open it. He had bought me a beautiful necklace with shells that I had seen a few days ago when we were looking around and a couple of things for our home. I smiled, gave him a hug, and told him I was so thankful that he was okay.

I told him I would dry out his sweaty clothes before packing them in the suitcase while he was in the shower. As I was drying them, I noticed a couple of drops of blood on his pants.

"Tom, are you sure you're okay?"

"Yeah why?"

"There's blood on your pants."

"Oh, I got a bloody nose while I was running. That happens sometimes. Must have dripped on my pants."

"Oh...okay," I said, but not 100% convinced.

He poked his head out of the shower and told me he was fine, just a little scared when they chased him.

I guess I believed him. He helped me finish packing the last of our things and we lay in bed for about thirty minutes before he fell asleep. Laying there, my mind was racing and I started thinking about the blood and his outbursts on this trip and even the girl at our wedding. Something seemed wrong – it all just didn't seem to make sense, but I couldn't put my finger on what was wrong. The last thing I wanted was to doubt my own husband, or even worse, be scared of him. As I closed my eyes, I concluded that these were likely isolated events and there was nothing connecting them but that didn't mean that I wasn't going to be a little guarded moving forward.

The next morning was bittersweet. We were leaving this beautiful resort but we were heading home to start our married life together. As we stood outside and waited for the airport bus, Tom went to the lobby to get us each a coffee. The bus arrived ten minutes later and we were off to the airport. As we got settled into our seats on the plane and I put my headphones on I started thinking about the past week. What an amazing honeymoon. Now we were heading home as newlyweds. I was so happy to have met Rachel. I hoped that I would see her again someday, or at least talk to her.

10

The Chase (At the Diner)

The girl behind the counter looked at me. "Do you have a phone?" I said louder. Her name tag said Molly.

"Are you okay?" she asked.

"He's coming. I need a phone," I said, gasping for air, "and a first aid kit."

She brought a phone out from behind the counter for me. I don't know why I didn't call the police, but my first thought was to dial Jessica. The phone rang about six times. "Why isn't she picking up," I thought to myself. Then I heard her voice.

"Hello?"

"Jess, it's me. Listen carefully. I'm at a diner near the train station, off Route 88 I think. He's after me. Jess, I'm scared, please hurry."

"Try to stay calm, I'm on my way." she said calmly.

Jess hung up and Molly asked me who was after me.

"Molly, where's your first aid kit?" I said frantically. "Do you have a back room I can use?"

"We have a staff room, you can go there. I'll show you." She escorted me to the staff room where they had a medical kit and a bench I could sit on. I was able to use a big cloth to wrap around my leg to help with the bleeding and used some tweezers to take out the pieces of glass in my feet. It hurt like hell pulling them out, but it hurt more walking with them sticking into me. I wrapped some gauze around my feet to help stop the bleeding. Molly had an extra pair of socks in her locker and gave them to me to help protect my feet. Unfortunately, she didn't have extra shoes, but the gauze and socks were a world of difference from the glass I had been running on.

While I was taking care of my feet, the cook in the back brought me a glass of water which I quickly guzzled. I don't think I'd drunk anything for hours and with all the running and lost blood, I was parched. I asked for a second glass as I didn't know when I would be able to drink again. Molly asked me whether I needed help and I told her my friend was on her way and would hopefully be here soon. She suggested we should call the police but I shook my head. It wasn't long after that we heard a car rolling up on the gravel road to the diner. Molly peeked her head out to see who it was and she told me it was a tall guy with dark hair and a baseball cap, walking toward the diner like he was on a mission.

"That's him," I said in a panic, "I need to get out of here."

Molly told the guy sitting in the booth to keep him busy and that I was never there.

As the door opened, I heard that same bell sound and my stomach went into knots. I could somewhat see from the back of the restaurant to the front as I peeked my head out from the staff room. He looked around and asked in a curious voice whether some girl had come in here recently. The guy in the booth said,

"We haven't seen any girl come through here in a while. What does she look like?"

The guy in the cap described me perfectly.

"Nope, haven't seen her. Maybe you should try down the road," the older man said. The guy in the booth glanced towards the kitchen and the man with the ball cap walked over to him, leaned over putting both of his hands down on the table the older guy was sitting at, looked him right in the eye, and said in a threatening tone "If you're lying to me, I suggest you don't."

"I don't want any trouble, sir. I'm just saying no girl came through here," the old guy replied calmly.

Molly walked out from the back of the restaurant toward the counter, about fifteen feet from the booth. The man leaning over, whipped his head up and he stared at her: I'm sure he thought it was me. I knew I had to get out of there or I would be a goner. Before I snuck out of the staff room, I grabbed the Swiss Army knife from the medical kit, just in case.

He walked up toward Molly and stood in front of the counter.

"I'm not asking again," he said in a lower and sterner voice. "Did the girl I described come by here recently?"

Molly was visibly shaking so he must have guessed that she had seen me or that she was withholding information about me. He took a step closer to her and that's when I tried to go out the back door and head toward the washrooms I had noticed when I got here.

"Where is she?" I heard him shout loudly.

"She's gone," Molly blurted as I went out the door.

I ran out the back and into the girls' washroom and climbed onto the toilet seat so my feet weren't showing. Not a moment later, I heard the bell sound again, which meant that someone must have walked into the restaurant, or someone had left. Then I heard a car door slam closed. Crouched on the toilet seat, I was shaking in fear.

Where was Jessica and why wasn't she here yet? Another minute went by and I wondered if he had left to try to find me so I carefully climbed down and came out of the stall to see if he was gone. I stepped out of the washrooms and when I peeked around the corner, I saw that the car was still there. My heart fell into my stomach.

As I turned to walk back toward the back door, somebody grabbed me from behind and put something over my mouth. It felt like a moist cloth. I fought and fought but the cloth stayed over my face and I could feel myself losing consciousness. He was pulling me toward the car and I could see that the trunk was open. I was so scared, but as I struggled I could feel myself getting weaker and weaker. I tried punching him but although my punches were landing, they were having no effect on him. I felt a blow to my cheek and as I fell to the ground, I could hear him yell at the people from the diner to mind their own business and go back inside. Weakened from whatever was on the cloth, coupled with having been hit, I could offer no resistance as he picked me up and dropped me into the trunk. I could hear voices, but I couldn't fight back. Just before I felt the thud of the trunk door being slammed down, I heard another vehicle skidding across the parking lot gravel.

"Jessica," I murmured, hoping desperately that it was her, but not having either the alertness or energy to make it louder. As the vehicle started moving, I lost consciousness.

11

New Beginnings

We landed back at home from our beautiful honeymoon and took a cab to our new house, our new home. It felt so good to be back as we had only been living in the house a couple of weeks so it still felt new to us. As we were both hungry and neither of us felt like cooking after a day of travelling, we ordered a pizza. I emptied our suitcases, threw a load of laundry in, and took a shower to freshen up. Sliding into your own bed after being away is the best feeling, no matter where you've been on vacation.

Tom joined me shortly after and we chatted about the trip and looked at our souvenirs. My bag was my favorite as I knew I would use it almost every day. I asked him what his favorite part was and he told me the fishing, even though it had gotten away just before he landed it on the boat, but he said at least he had the picture to remember his near triumph. For me, I told him it was probably the catamaran and seeing a whale because it is rare and something I had always wanted to see. I omitted the times spent with Rachel and Paul as I didn't want to ruin the moment. By now it was quite late and we were both tired from the long day and decided to pack it in.

The next day we went over to Brad and Taylor's to get our house key back and also see how things were while we were gone. As we approached the head of their driveway, we could see them through the upstairs window, half naked and making out. We started laughing but figured we would come back later when they weren't busy. We went home to do some organizing and cleaning. We hadn't had time before we left for the honeymoon to unpack and put everything away and we both had to start back at work in two days. Just before we left for our honeymoon, I had landed a full-time job as a secretary at a counselling office about fifteen minutes from our house. The job would pay fairly well and allow me to get my foot in the door for when I finished my Master's. I was even going to be allowed to sit in on some sessions because I had a basic certification that allowed me to observe and provide feedback, but just not diagnose yet.

Tom had started a tech company while in his final year of school and he was actually doing quite well. It also gave him the freedom to work from home and be on his own schedule. We had to paint a couple of the rooms as they were not attractive colors when we bought the place, but nothing a couple of gallons of paint couldn't fix. We spent most of the morning and early afternoon painting the two rooms and then thought we would try going to Brad and Taylor's again while the paint dried. We headed over there and this time there was no show from the driveway. Tom rang the doorbell and Taylor answered the door. We were invited in for lemonade and chatted about the past week. Tom and I asked how their morning was going and we gave each other a knowing smirk.

Brad said that he had cut our grass and put our sprinkler on a couple of times as there was some pretty hot weather while we were away. They asked us about our honeymoon and I gave them all the details, well most of them anyway. Of course I left out the incident where Tom raged at Paul as I didn't think it was important to our honeymoon story and it didn't put Tom in the best light. I did most of the talking, but Taylor jumped in and asked Tom whether he had enjoyed the trip. At one point, she even looked at him and said, point blank, "So did you guys have lots of honeymoon sex?" Both Tom and I almost choked on our drinks, not expecting such a question. Brad rolled his eyes in embarrassment of her question. We both smiled and I replied, "We had a great time, that's all I'm saying." I didn't really feel comfortable sharing my intimate moments with my husband to a neighbor I have only known for a week, but I did want her to know that I am more than capable of meeting his needs.

Changing the topic, Brad mentioned that they were having a party the following week and invited us to come. Before I could respond that we would have to let them know, Tom spoke up and said "Sounds great. We'll be there." I looked at him and said, "Sure, we'd love to come," but I wasn't as eager as Tom. "We should go" I mouthed to Tom as I wanted to finish cleaning the house, but also feeling uncomfortable at Taylor's forwardness and her flirtiness towards Tom. Maybe it was just her personality to be bubbly and nice, but my gut was telling me there was more to it.

As we were walking home, I asked Tom if he thought Taylor was flirting with him and he told me I was being ridiculous. "She's married, Kerry. You just need to relax. She just asked about our honeymoon because that's what people do on their honeymoon."

"Still, it's more than a bit nosy to be asking about such a thing, don't you think?" I replied.

"You're reading into it," he sighed back.

"Well I still think she was looking at you with wandering eyes."

"Well that sucks for her then because I'm all yours," he said. That made me smile.

As we started cleaning again, Tom thought it would be funny to grab a paint brush and daub paint on my forehead. I was a little shocked but I decided to play along. I grabbed the other wet brush and swiped it across his cheek. At this point we were in a full-out paint war, wrestling and trying to paint each other. A couple of minutes of that went by before he grabbed my arms and put them over my head and kissed me, with our faces and hair full of paint. I could even feel paint down my shirt, but at that moment I didn't care. He started kissing my stomach and then took off my pants, kissing my hips and thighs. Then he made love to me right there on the bedroom floor on top of the drop cloths we had put down to protect the floor from paint. I loved his spontaneity. I took a shower and got all the paint out of my hair, then made dinner for us while he finished putting stuff away.

That night we almost had all the house cleaned up and decided to relax the next day as we both started back to work the day after. I was looking forward to the new job, but things would be a bit different as we wouldn't see each other as much as we had the past few weeks. That's okay because they say space is good for a marriage.

Monday came and I woke up before Tom as I had to be at the clinic by 8:00 and didn't want to be late my first day. I got settled in and met some of the therapists. My boss showed me around and was very helpful in making sure I had everything I needed to start. His name was Rob. He was about ten years older than me, but quite attractive. Not that I looked at him like that, but it's hard not to notice when someone is good looking.

I took some calls in the morning and processed some payments for clients' sessions. Around lunch-time Rob offered to take me to lunch to welcome me and discuss how things were going so far. He asked me about my future schooling and professional plans and also a bit about my personal life, but he didn't pry. I told him I had just gotten married and that's why I had needed the week off before I started as that was my honeymoon. In the interview, I hadn't said anything about the honeymoon because I hadn't thought it was pertinent: rather I had told them that I had a pre-booked trip and I wasn't able to start until I had returned.

We had a nice lunch and he also told me that he had a wife and a two-year-old girl. He seemed like a great guy to work for and seemed interested in seeing me succeed. He told me he was always looking to mentor therapists and that when I finished my Master's, there would be a coun-selling position for me. I thanked him for that and for lunch and we headed back to the office where I finished my workday.

When I got home, Tom was sitting at his computer at the kitchen table. He asked me how my first day had been and I told him all about it. I told him how great my colleagues were and how my boss was so great to work for and had even taken me out for lunch. Tom's eyebrows somewhat creased in uneasy annoyance that my boss had invited me out for lunch, but I quickly told him it was a welcome to the team thing and he was married and had a child. The eyebrows somewhat uncreased at that but I could tell he was still perturbed. I told Tom how Rob had told me that there would be a position as a counsellor for me once I completed my Master's and Tom responded with a slightly enthusiastic, "That's good".

"You should be happy for me," I retorted in frustration, "It's a big opportunity for my career." I left the kitchen and went upstairs to our room to change, eager to avoid a fight and frustrated by his lack of support.

I came back down shortly afterwards to start making supper and while I was in the kitchen Tom walked up behind me and put his arms around my waist and said "Kerry, I'm sorry I wasn't more supportive. I am happy for you as I know this is what you want to do. I guess I just thought it was odd that your boss wanted to take you, and only you, out for lunch on your first day."

"Oh stop being jealous," I said lightheartedly with a smile, "Like I said, he's married and probably 10 years older."

"I just can't help myself. I don't know what I would do if anyone tried to take you away from me," he said in a somewhat serious tone.

"You have nothing to worry about. Now help me with dinner," I instructed him with a smile on my face.

The rest of the week was pretty much the same. I went to work, met Tom for lunch at a nearby cafe, and then went home. Most times he was home when I got there: sometimes he was out for a jog. We had finished decorating the house, but like any new couple there were still things we wanted to do, but needed some time and money to be able to finish everything.

We had that party to go to at Brad and Taylor's which I was still somewhat on the fence about, but they were our closest neighbors so I figured, 'what the hell'. Tom thought it would be nice to bring a bottle of wine so we went into town to grab a couple of bottles.

Taylor opened the door when we arrived and you could tell she had already had a few drinks. She was even bubblier than usual and grabbed Tom's arm and told us to come in while pulling Tom in. I had a feeling this was going to be a long night. Brad came down the stairs and said with a grin "She's been into the wine already," and laughed. With my half-fake smile I replied "Well that's what parties are for, right?"

"She's a handful that's for sure," Brad shot back.

He invited us out back where the rest of the guests were so we could meet them. As we walked through their house, I noticed how modern and expensive the decor was. "He certainly must have money," I thought. As we got near the back door, I noticed there was a large group outside, possible twenty or twenty-five. That was a much larger group than I had been expecting. I wasn't crazy about large groups, but didn't let it get to me. Brad introduced us and Taylor was still hanging onto Tom's arm like they were best friends. I knew she was a bit tipsy and just being friendly, but seriously. I didn't want to come across as jealous, so I just asked Tom if he could help me by opening the bottle of wine. I thought this would at least make Miss Grabby Hands let go and give him his arm back.

Tom opened the wine and we started mingling with others at the party. Brad had great food on the BBQ and plenty for everyone to drink. About two hours had passed when I suddenly noticed Tom was nowhere to be seen. I looked around to see where Taylor was but she was also MIA. I looked back into the house and I saw her walk into the kitchen and she came up and appeared to say something in Tom's ear. I had had enough. I briskly walked into the house and said, "What's going on here?" Tom spun around quickly and said "Nothing. Taylor was just thanking us for coming to her party."

Taylor piped up and said "Relax, it's a party. Have a drink. He wasn't doing anything."

"You've had enough to drink for both of us," I mumbled back. I don't think she heard me, but she glanced at me once more, then walked back outside to rejoin the party.

"Was that what she really said Tom?" I asked.

"Yeah, what else would it be?" he replied.

"I don't know, you tell me. She seems awfully fond of you, especially your arm."

"She's just outgoing. You need to relax." He grabbed another bottle of wine off the counter and walked outside.

We stayed for about another hour, talking with other guests and Taylor kept her distance, but she glanced at Tom now and then while talking to others.

Finally I told Tom I was tired and was going to head back to the house. He seemed to want to stay, but offered to leave with me. When we got back to the house I let Tom know how I felt.

"You embarrassed me in front of those people."

"Who?" he asked.

"You know who. Taylor. You seem so oblivious that she is practically throwing herself at you." I said in frustration.

Then Tom took a step toward me and said in a tone I had never heard before, "I don't like being questioned, and don't need my wife acting like an insecure child. So is this going to be a problem?"

I was in total shock. I couldn't believe what and how he had said it. I couldn't say anything except to give a squeaky one-word response. "No."

He walked upstairs to take a shower. That was not the Tom I knew who loved and respected me. It filled me with disquiet and apprehension: how could he talk to me that way? And why?

I decided to take a bubble bath in the other bathroom and try and relax from what had just happened. As I lay there in the tub, tears ran down my face. That was not the man I had married. I sure hoped that wasn't a glimpse of our future together. I was in the tub when Tom tapped on the door and walked into the bathroom. He sat on the toilet and looked at me.

"I'm sorry I said what I did. I shouldn't have used that tone. Can you forgive me?"

I honestly didn't know what to think or say. I couldn't just forget what he had said or how he had said it. With a forced smile, I hollowly responded "I forgive you," in a soft voice.

"Good. I love you Kerry and would never hurt you." He kissed me on the forehead and left the room. Shortly after, I got out, dried myself off, put on my pajamas, and went to bed.

The next morning I had planned to go for a jog. Just as I was leaving, Tom asked whether he could join me. I didn't object as I thought perhaps this would help us move past what had happened the previous night. He seemed to be in an energetic mood: I was still unsure what to feel about what had happened. I know love is about forgiveness, but it's hard when something like that is said. I guess I just had to see how he acted going forward.

During our jog Tom tried to engage me in conversation a few times. Each time I replied briefly in order to not make it awkward. He even squirted water at me from his bottle to make me laugh. Although I was a little annoyed, I did crack a smile. As we approached our driveway, Tom stopped me by gently grabbing my arm so I faced him.

"I can tell you're still bothered by last night. I am truly sorry Kerry. I love you."

His words made me feel a little better, but part of me was still struggling because I had never seen that side of him before. Had he been putting on a show the past couple of years and now that we were married, were these his true colors finally showing?

"I love you too, but you scared me," I replied.

"I know, and that's the last thing I ever wanted to do. It won't happen again."

Tom saw that I had a tear running down my cheek and wiped it for me. Then he gave me a big hug and I wrapped my arms around him. We stood there for a couple of minutes just holding each other. I wanted to believe him. We headed inside and he said he would make breakfast and I could go shower and relax if I wanted. I didn't object as I was sweaty from the run and thought a nice shower would make me feel better.

When I came downstairs, he was cooking up a storm. I sat at the island, he handed me a cappuccino and I watched him cook. While sitting there, I brought up the idea of having a housewarming, as I knew other people who'd had one, I thought maybe we ought to as well. He actually liked the idea so we discussed it for a while, details such as who to invite and what kind of housewarming party to throw. We decided we would have it a couple of weeks later so we could give guests plenty of notice and so that we would have lots of time to pick up everything we would need.

Planning the party with Tom actually made me feel more comfortable, like we were returning to our normal rhythm again as I tried to forgive him and put that time behind us. After breakfast, we sat in deck chairs on the patio and ironed out the rest of the details and guest list. Tom even suggested inviting my boss. My guess is that he was just trying to be supportive, but I appreciated the effort nevertheless. I thought we should also invite some of the therapists as we didn't know a lot of people in the area and it would be good to make some new friends. Of course Jessica and Calvin were obviously going to have to be there as we hadn't seen them for several weeks. Tom invited the one guy he had working for him and his close friend who had been at our wedding.

A little reluctant to invite Brad and Taylor because of the incident at their party, I agreed they should be invited so that we could hopefully move past it. We also decided to go outside of our usual group and invite our other neighbors who we hadn't yet met so that we could get to know more people. We also were able to get ahold of a few other friends from college who all said they could make it. In total I think we were expecting about twenty to twenty-five people so a pretty good number. Now all we needed were decorations, food, and alcohol.

The next couple of weeks went by fairly quickly as I was working full time and starting my online schooling for my Master's in the evenings. Tom was busy with his work as well, but we managed time for dinner together and the occasional movie night. I was really enjoying my job and on the Friday before our housewarming party, I got to sit in on my first session with Shelley, one of the therapists. She had been doing therapy for about ten years and was very good at it: she could read people very well.

That night I came home after observing my first session and was so excited to tell Tom and he seemed happy for me. I couldn't provide names because of client-patient confidentiality but I did give him some details. The client was caught in a dilemma with himself because he had cheated on his wife and felt horrible about it, but he felt he might do it again. He didn't want to tell her and ruin his marriage. Shelley figured the guy might even have a sex addiction and discussed strategies to help him. Tom thought it was interesting how some people seemed to be living double lives and how their loved ones had no clue what was going on. I told Tom that some people are very good at deception, lacking the ability to feel remorse for their actions and their impact on others. He told me he couldn't understand how someone could act in such dissimilar ways without anyone recognizing the different behaviors.

I decided to move on from that topic because he didn't seem to appreciate the psychology behind this client's behavior: either that or he was just playing dumb.

I figured that we had better set up tables and bowls for the party the next evening and do some last-minute cleaning so the house looked presentable for our guests. Tom offered to help, which was nice and allowed me to be done sooner. To show my appreciation I asked whether he wanted to join me in a nice hot bath. We hadn't been intimate in over two weeks. With all the drama, coupled with work and school, there had been little free time and my mood, naturally enough, wasn't there. He accepted my offer and we had a relaxing time, enjoying glasses of wine together. Although we didn't have sex that night, just being in the bath together and lying in bed afterwards, cuddling one another was a step back toward creating balance in our relationship.

The next day was our housewarming and everything looked amazing. Guests started arriving around 4:00 and many brought a bottle of wine or some other gift. We had our guests place them on the kitchen table, waiting to be opened later. Tom was a great host, ensuring everyone who showed up had a drink of their choice in hand, while I conducted tours around the house.

I was extremely excited to see Jess and Calvin as she was my closest friend and I hadn't seen her in a while. They brought us a gift and because it was Jess, I wanted to open it right away, plus it was huge so I was very curious. It was a beautiful large clock for our wall and Tom seemed pleased with it. Jessica and I grabbed drinks and she helped me with some of the snacks in the kitchen while Tom and Calvin went outside to start barbecuing. Jessica asked how things were going as newlyweds and everything with us. I told her things were going pretty well, except I felt that I had to tell her about the incident with Tom. She was shocked and told me that I should at least be aware of other signs of that repeating itself and to not ignore them. Jessica was like a sister to me as we had become very close while we shared a dorm room in college, so she was quite protective of me. I told her about my new job and she was so happy for me. I also told her how Tom thought my boss was hitting on me because he took me out for lunch. She thought that was absurd and said so.

"What's his deal? Why is he acting so jealous all of a sudden?"

"I don't know. I haven't given him any reason to be. He's not the Tom I met in college, that's for sure."

"Well, you let me know if you need anything, girl. I'm always here for you and I just want you to be happy."

"I'm happy, just lately things have been different and it kind of bothers me as there shouldn't be any issues like this already."

"Well I'm just saying, if things were to get worse, you would need to get out and look after yourself,"

"I know. I don't think it would get to that point, at least I hope not. We did just get married not that long ago."

"Okay, well just remember I'm just a phone call away." Jess concluded. We grabbed some of the extra snacks and brought them out to the backyard.

Everyone seemed to have showed up, even Brad and bubbly Taylor. I figured I would try to be nice to avoid any more drama. She was actually nice to me, but I wasn't quite sure if it was just because it was our housewarming or because she had actually put our little scuffle behind us. She brought us a couple of bottles of wine and a card that said "to our new neighbors. Our home is always open for you. If you ever need anything, just give us a call." It was a nice gesture, but I didn't plan on calling her. Tom thanked them both when he read the card and told them they should have our phone number too in case of an emergency. He gave his cell phone number to them. I wasn't sure they needed it but I guessed it could be useful in the event of an emergency. Tom then went back to check on his BBQ.

Everyone seemed to be enjoying themselves. Rob and Shelley came up to chat with Jess and me at one point and I noticed Tom glancing over our way. A couple of minutes later, Tom made his way over and introduced himself to Rob and Shelley. He seemed to be kind of measuring Rob up but shook his hand and thanked him for coming even so. Rob told Tom how great an addition to his team I was and that I would make a great therapist one day. While looking at me and then back at Rob, he said, "Yeah she's pretty amazing," to which I smiled and felt a little embarrassed.

Then Tom asked Rob about his family and counselling experience. It almost seemed like he was having Rob reiterate that he was married and had a family – facts Tom already knew because I had told him. Rob told Tom about his wife and little daughter, to which Tom responded, "Well it sounds like you have a beautiful family." I caught Shelley's eye but she didn't say anything. I could tell by her look that she was trying to get a read on Tom. Tom excused himself to go check on the burgers. Rob said that Tom seemed to be a nice guy, but I could tell he was trying to be nice and downplay the awkwardness he had felt talking to Tom.

As the evening wore on, I spent a lot of time visiting with Jess and Calvin, and Tom hung out mostly with his close friend. The other neighbors we had invited seemed nice, but they were a little older than us. My guess was that they were in their 40s. They seemed to gravitate around Rob and a couple of therapists who were talking to him, likely because they all seemed around the same age. Those neighbors didn't stay overly late.

The rest of us continued to drink and visit and things seemed to be going well. Well enough anyway, until I caught sight of Taylor sitting next to Tom and chatting away. Normally I wouldn't care if someone talked to Tom, but she was a little too forward in my opinion. I was talking to Shelley at the time and we both looked over and at one point Taylor leaned in and seemed to be whispering in Tom's ear. Shelley even made a comment that Taylor seemed a bit flirtatious. I told her it wasn't the first time she had acted this way to which Shelley responded with "Oh, I'm sure it's nothing." Her response did not satisfy my concerns. I considered going over to them to interrupt their conversation when I saw Jess walk over to them. She looked deadly serious and said something to Tom and then looked at Taylor. Almost immediately, Taylor got up and walked away and Tom gave Jess a sour look. She came over to where Shelley and I were standing and I asked her what she had said to cause Taylor to get up and walk away so quickly.

"I just told her that maybe she should spend more time talking to her husband than whispering in some married man's ear as it comes across as slutty," said Jess. I snickered but realized that I would likely be getting blowback from Tom later that evening.

"Thanks Jess," I replied.

"Well someone needed to say something," she responded, "Don't need no homewrecker around here," she added in a serious tone but then smiled. Tom and Jess had never seemed to have any issues before, as we all gotten along, but I could tell by the look on Tom's face that Jessica's actions did not sit well with him.

About forty five minutes went by and other guests started heading out. Jess and Calvin hung around a bit longer to help clean up. As they were standing by the door getting ready to leave, she took a step towards Tom and said quietly, but loud enough so that I could hear, "Treat her right," then she faced me and told me to call her so we could get together soon and turned around and walked out the door with Calvin. Tom shut the door and then looked at me as if I had had something to do with Jess's comments. "She should mind her own business," he said, then he walked upstairs.

That night we didn't talk much as I could tell he was still annoyed. I was tired from the party and cleaning so I ended up going to bed without saying much more to him than thanking him for his help and asking him if he had a good time. His response was fairly terse, indicating that he had had an okay time and was glad his friend was able to make it.

The next day I woke up a little later than usual and Tom was walking through the front door all sweaty as I came down the stairs. He must have gotten up early and gone for a jog. He was in a better mood and asked whether I wanted to go into town for breakfast, which I thought was a nice gesture and agreed to. We had a good conversation at the cafe, but on the way home Tom asked why Jessica had acted that way. He asked me whether I had said anything to her. I paused. I wasn't sure that I should tell him the truth, but then again lying wouldn't be good either.

"She just asked me how things were going and I told her what had happened with Taylor that time. She's my best friend and we tell each other everything." Tom's facial expression was not a happy one.

"I would appreciate if you kept our relationship issues between us," he said sternly but calmly.

"I didn't mean to start anything, I was just upset," I replied.

"If you have a problem, talk to me," he said in frustration.

"Okay, I'm sorry," I said soberly. The rest of the drive home was quiet.

I just did some house-cleaning and laundry, and worked on my schooling a bit the rest of that day. I wanted to get to bed early as I had to work the next day.

Before bed Tom peeked his head into the office where I was working on my courses and said "Kerry, sorry I got upset earlier. I just don't like people prying into our personal life and want us to talk about things, that's all."

"Okay," I replied.

"Goodnight." Tom answered and left to go to bed. I appreciated his apology, but I was starting to see a trend of him getting upset, apologizing, and repeating it all over again.

The next day I got to work early and Rob had brought coffee in for everyone which I thought was nice. Usually Rob and some of the therapists would gather around my desk to chat for a few minutes before the day got underway. Shelley and Rob were both there and thanked me again for inviting them to the party and I thanked them for the wine and gifts. Shelley looked like she wanted to say something else, but was quiet. I asked her what was on her mind and she proceeded to tell me that she had watched Tom and was a little concerned at his behavior.

She said "I know it might not be my place, Kerry, as I've only known you a short time but since we work together and I care about everybody on our staff, I feel I should give my opinion. Your husband seemed quite jealous at the party and even seemed like he was about to freak out on Rob when we were talking. I have seen this before with clients. They are controlling and have anger issues which can result in unpredictable and potentially aggressive behaviors. No disrespect to your husband, but I am just saying be mindful of this, okay?"

"Thanks for your concern, but Tom would never hurt me."

"That's what many women think….until it's too late."

"He did seem quite annoyed with me for some reason, Kerry," Rob chimed in, "I hope it won't be a problem for you to work with us?"

"No, not at all," I replied, trying as much to convince myself as them.

I couldn't believe that even my coworkers had seen that side of him. Now I was feeling embarrassed that they had seen my husband as a control freak with a temper. I thought about what to say, but nothing I could say would make any difference. "I'll watch to see if it gets worse," is all I could offer. We went about the rest of our day and I was able to sit in on another session later that afternoon.

The rest of the week was quite busy with work and school, and Tom was busy getting more clients for his business. We still had dinner together every night and good conversation when we lay in bed together. I planned on going shopping with Jessica on the weekend to spend some girl time together. Tom said he was going to do some yard work and mentioned building me a garden, which I thought was quite nice of him. The next day Jessica pulled up the driveway to take me shopping and Tom was outside. As I came out of the house Jessica rolled down the window and greeted Tom, but he looked up briefly at her and put his head back down and continued raking the lawn. I got in and we drove away.

"What's his problem?" Jess asked.

"Oh he's probably just still sour because you called him out."

"Good, maybe he shouldn't act like a tool and let floozies throw themselves at him."

I kind of chuckled at her comment because I agreed with her. We had a great time shopping and when she dropped me off, we made plans to meet for lunch the following week.

That night Tom and I had a movie night together. I admit that I had missed the intimacy, but it's hard to be that way with someone who acted as he had at the party. That being said, I wanted to reconnect with him so I tried to make the first move while we were watching our movie. He was receptive to my advances and it started great, but this time he was a little rougher and quicker in his loving towards me. It kind of felt a little like he just wanted a quick fix rather than the slow and intimate moments we'd shared before. He went up to bed shortly after and I lay there, alone on the couch. I was a little bothered, but it had been a while for us so maybe he had just been in the heat of the moment. I thought about it some more, trying not to read too much into it, and fell asleep on the couch.

Monday came, which meant another long week. While I was at work, Tom showed up. He had never come to my workplace before and his timing couldn't have been worse. Rob was standing behind me at my desk, somewhat leaning with one hand on my chair and the other on my desk looking at my computer. He was helping me with the scheduling calendar. It was completely innocent, but to Tom this was a little too close for comfort.

"Oh, hey Tom," Rob said enthusiastically.

"Hey," Tom said back briefly.

Turning to me, he said, "I thought I could take you for lunch."

I looked to Rob for approval, "Sure, go ahead," he said.

I took my purse out of my desk drawer and we headed out the door.

As we drove to the restaurant Tom said, "Your boss sure likes to get close to his employees, hey."

"What do you mean?" I asked.

"The way he was standing, hovering over you like that. He's probably trying to sneak a peek."

"What are you talking about?" I said in disbelief.

"I told you he's married."

"Well that doesn't mean anything. I bet he'd love to get in your pants."

"Excuse me?" I said disgusted. "I don't even want to go to lunch with you."

He stopped the car on the side of the road.

"Sorry, I didn't mean that," he replied. "I just see the way he was looking at you and I didn't like it."

"Well it doesn't matter if you don't like it. There's nothing to like. First of all, he's my boss and secondly, is that what you think I am? Some slut who's going to sleep with her boss?"

"Of course not," he replied.

"Then you need to stop with your accusations and jealousy," I demanded.

Tom kind of smiled and put his hand on my thigh, "I'm sorry, can we still go for lunch?"

I paused.

"I guess so," I said, frustrated. "You drive me crazy sometimes," I added.

We went for lunch, but I wasn't in a talkative mood after his comments, even if he had apologized. He tried to engage me in a conversation, asking me how work was going. I gave brief answers so there wouldn't be total silence. I only had about forty minutes for lunch and then Tom took me back to work. As I walked into the clinic, Rob was standing by the door.

"Everything okay?" he asked.

"I'm fine," I said, trying not to show my irritation as it would only make him think worse of Tom and that I was in a bad relationship.

I looked out the window and could see Tom staring at Rob as if to show his dislike for him. Rob looked back at him for a second and then walked away from the door.

I tried to concentrate on my job the rest of the afternoon, but was so angry at Tom for having acted like that. What the hell was his problem? The guy I met in college, my loving and sweet Tom was not like that anymore. He was becoming more and more jealous and controlling as time went on and it all seemed to have started when we got married. Maybe Jessica and Shelley were right. If this didn't change, I might have to reconsider whether my marriage was worth saving.

That night Tom had made dinner for me when I got home, but I knew he was just doing it to suck up. He apologized again at dinner, but I was too annoyed to totally forgive him. After supper I spent most of the night in the home office studying and waiting for him to go to bed first.

Two days later Jessica texted me in the morning to confirm our lunch date. I said yes, but asked whether she could pick up my purse at the house as I had forgotten it by the door when I had left for work. She told me it would be no problem and would pick me up after she had grabbed it.

When she arrived at my office, I got in the car and she had a funny smirk on her face. I asked her what was so funny and she proceeded to tell me that when she had been driving up toward the house, she had passed Taylor and Brad's house. She said that she could see Taylor's naked back pressed up against an upstairs window and Brad making love to her. She couldn't see his face, just her naked ass and long hair. Immediately my stomach knotted.

"What's wrong?" she asked as she could see I looked uneasy.

"Brad had told us he was heading out of town this week," I replied.

"You don't think?" Jessica's voice changed.

"He had better not be screwing that bitch. We need to go there now!"

Jessica sped up and headed towards our place which was about fifteen minutes away. I tried calling Tom's cell and there was no answer: I was trembling.

As we pulled up to Taylor's house, I stormed up to the door, pounding on it. After ten or twelve times, the door opened and there was Taylor.

"Where is he?" I demanded.

"Where is who?" she replied dumbfounded.

"Tom. He's here, isn't he?"

"I don't know what you're talking about," she replied.

"Where's your husband?" I asked.

"He left a little while ago for a business trip," she replied.

I walked into her house and called out for Tom. There was just dead silence.

"You'd better hope he wasn't here," I said threateningly.

"You need to calm down. He's probably at home or out for a run," she replied. I didn't appreciate her telling me to calm down, but maybe I had jumped the gun a bit with my accusations. The timing just didn't seem right.

I asked Jessica if she was sure she hadn't seen who the guy by the window was. She confirmed she hadn't been able to make out who it was but had just naturally assumed it was Brad. My animosity toward Taylor and her flirtatious behavior made me doubt her candor about Tom not having been there, but I was almost certain that Brad had said he was leaving early in the morning. "I'm losing my mind," I thought.

I asked Jessica to head straight to our place to see whether Tom was there. We pulled up and I walked through the house, calling frantically for him, but I couldn't find him. I went out to the backyard and there he was, wearing headphones and mowing the lawn. I tapped him on the shoulder and he nearly jumped out of his skin. He took the headphones off and I asked him where he had been all morning.

He looked confused at what I was asking. "I've been here working and took a break to mow the lawn."

"You haven't been anywhere else?"

"No, like where?" he asked. He seemed to be pretty sincere the way he had responded. I didn't tell him I had barged into Taylor's house as he would just think I was a jealous nutcase, especially after I had called him out for his jealousy, even though I felt my suspicions were more legitimate.

Jessica walked into the backyard shortly thereafter and gave Tom a look of deep loathing. He rolled his eyes at her and went back to mowing. I told Jess that maybe I was just paranoid. I had seen how flirty Taylor was with Tom and knowing Brad had left earlier for his business trip, I thought that Taylor had texted Tom and he had come running. I didn't have anything except my suspicions: I would just have to take his word for it that nothing had happened.

That night as we lay in bed, I told Tom I was sorry for having come home all panicky, for having believed Taylor had contacted him for some fling because Jessica saw her and a guy in the window, and for the whole misunderstanding. He laughed and said, "So you thought I was the guy in the window, and this is without Jessica even seeing who it was? You just assumed I would cheat on you?"

"No…well, I just thought maybe because we haven't been connecting lately and Taylor keeps throwing herself at you…I don't know. Sorry I'm just being suspicious."

"You're right, you're being paranoid. I'm going to sleep." He turned over and a few minutes later I heard snoring.

The next day I was very busy at work and before I knew it the day was nearly over. Rob and I both walked out together and Rob's mouth dropped as he looked at his car. A knife was sticking out of his front driver side tire and it was completely flat. I immediately thought, 'even that would be too far for Tom.' Sometimes clients can do vengeful things if they thing they are not being taken seriously or are not being heard, but for Tom to do this because he didn't like my boss would be too much. We both looked at it, then Rob pulled out his cell phone to phone a tow truck.

When I got home, I told Tom about what had happened and all he said was, "Wow, he must have really pissed off someone a lot." I was mystified by his comment. I wondered whether he had done it, but I didn't want to make any more accusations after the whole Taylor incident.

"He was pretty mad that someone would do that to his car. Someone's obviously unhinged," I said and looked at Tom to see his reaction. His expression didn't change.

The next couple of weeks were fairly regular: busy work days, normal home life. I would come home from work at my usual time and on a couple of occasions, I saw Tom jogging on the road between Brad's house and ours, but didn't think anything of it for the most part, as he went jogging almost daily. Admittedly I did slow down as I passed their house on occasion to see if there were any more surprises in the window. He and I were getting along fairly well and there didn't seem to be any drama. One Friday, Brad phoned and invited us over for dinner the next day. I accepted, never imagining that this get-together would change everything.

12

Secrets Revealed

Tom and I got dressed to go for dinner and he grabbed a bottle of wine to bring with us. We rang the doorbell and Taylor answered. She was quite welcoming to both of us and seemed less flirty with Tom. Brad had invited us to dinner so that he could share some big news with us. He got everyone a drink while we arranged ourselves on the sofa. He then told us that he just gotten back from his business trip and wanted us to be the first to know that Taylor was pregnant. We were both surprised.

I looked at Tom and he seemed happy for them, but he also seemed quite shocked. I congratulated them both. Hearing such happy news made me feel better because maybe she really was just bubbly and friendly, not promiscuous after all. We sat down to eat and after supper, I offered to help Taylor with the dishes before we had dessert, while the guys went for a beer in the basement.

Taylor and I discussed her pregnancy and she mentioned she was only a few weeks into it, but was excited for her first child. I told her I was looking forward to having kids too, but wanted to wait a couple of years until I had finished my schooling. Anything she needed during the next few months, I told her I would be there for her. Maybe we could finally become friends.

After we had had dessert and coffee, I told her I needed to freshen up and excused myself. I decided to use the upstairs one as I hadn't seen their upstairs the previous time we had been there. Admittedly I was more than a little curious, so I slowly walked into their bedroom to look around and as I gently slid my feet across the floor, I felt my toes hit something. I looked down and my mouth fell open and I felt like throwing up. Right there on the floor near the bed was the gold 'K' that I had given Tom for his keychain. What the hell was it doing here? It must have been Tom that Jessica had seen through the window. "I can't believe this is happening to me," I thought and then suddenly, like a bolt of lightning, I wondered, "Was the baby Tom's?" A soul-destroying rage suddenly and violently welled up inside me like an erupting volcano.

I walked back downstairs, grabbed my coat from the coat tree, and told Brad that I wasn't feeling well and was going home. Tom followed me out and asked me to stop, but I kept walking. He continued to follow me and then grabbed my arm to stop me. I yelled at him, "Let me go, you despicable son-of-a-bitch. I believed you when you said you would never do that to me."

"What are you talking about?" he asked, apparently bewildered.

"I found this in their bedroom," holding the 'K' up to his face.

He looked like a deer in the headlights and turned as pale as a sheet.

Brad and Taylor were standing outside, but I wasn't sure they could hear us as we were already at the end of their driveway.

"You whore!" I yelled toward Taylor and turned to continue walking back home. Tom walked behind me until we were almost at the house. I unlocked the door and flung it open. He followed me in and slammed the door. I turned around to yell at him some more when he suddenly grabbed my arms and pushed me up against the wall.

"Who the hell do you think you are? Making a scene like that in front of the neighbors!"

"Let go of me," I demanded.

"You walk around here ignoring me half the time, what did you expect?"

My anger was replaced by shock and fear.

"I expect you to be faithful," I replied with tears in my eyes.

"Well you married me for better or worse."

"That doesn't include you cheating on your wife."

"It's not like it meant anything, it was just sex. Get over it." He let go and walked away. I slid down the wall to the floor, sobbing uncontrollably.

It was like he had no remorse and acted as if it was my fault. I walked upstairs to our bedroom and shut the door. I was full-blown crying by now and phoned Jessica to tell her what had happened. She was so pissed off and wanted to drive over right then and there to kick his ass, but I told her that would only make matters worse. I must have cried for an hour straight that night. How had we ended up like this? Why had he done this to me? We had been so happy. I didn't want to get a divorce already, become another statistic, but I also wasn't going to accept or allow him to cheat on me and be okay with it. I needed some time to think about things before I made any decisions.

The next week was very rough. I had difficulties concentrating at work and Rob and Shelley could tell something was wrong. One day while leaving the office, Rob gave me a friendly hug while I was leaving. I had told him what I was going through. He was just trying to be a good friend. That night when I got home Tom asked how my day was and then told me that Rob had better watch himself or something could happen to him. I had to assume that Tom was watching me now to see what I was doing during the day, maybe thinking I would be trying to get back at him for cheating on me. I wasn't like that. I told Tom I didn't know what he was talking about to which he just laughed and said that I had been warned. The old Tom would never have acted like this. He was a completely different person now, someone I barely recognized, or wanted to for that matter.

Two days later, around lunch time we got a call at work from Rob's wife. He had been in an accident and the police said foul play was involved because there was something wrong with his car brakes. She said he was badly injured but would pull through. I started freaking out because I was almost certain Tom had done it. I went to the hospital to see Rob and he was in rough shape. His left eye was swollen shut, he had a cast on his right arm, and lacerations and cuts on his face. After a few minutes of being there, he opened his right eye and I began to cry. I told him how sorry I was. I heard him say quietly but firmly, "It's not your fault." Then he said, a little bit louder, "Leave before he hurts you too," and then dozed off again.

I left his room and headed for home so Tom wouldn't wonder where I was. I texted Jessica and asked whether I could stay at her place so I could have some space from Tom and of course she didn't mind at all. I texted Tom that I was out running some errands and would be back later. Jessica and Calvin made me dinner and we chatted about what had happened. They both told me they were worried about me and expressed their shock and disapproval at Tom's behavior. They told me I could stay there as long as I needed. A few hours went by and I received a text from Tom.

"Where are you?" I didn't want to answer so I didn't reply. Ten minutes later, "Where are you?" Three minutes later, "Where the hell are you and why aren't you replying?" Finally I answered as I could tell he was getting upset.

"I'm at Jessica's. I'm staying the night."

"You sure you want to do that?" he texted back. It sounded more like a threat than a question.

"I'll see you tomorrow." I replied, then muted my phone.

The next day I called in sick to work as I didn't feel the best and wanted to spend more time with Jessica. Just after breakfast Tom showed up and knocked on the door.

Calvin answered and Tom said, "Where is she?"

"She's upstairs with Jessica. Maybe you should calm down and go home Tom," Calvin suggested.

"This isn't your concern" Tom responded angrily, trying to look past Calvin to see if he could see me.

"Kerry!" Tom shouted for me. I didn't know if I should go downstairs or stay put. I didn't want to involve Jessica and Calvin in the situation. Jessica told me to stay in the room while she went down to talk to him. She went to the door and stood behind Calvin and said "You're a bastard. What kind of man cheats on his wife?" Apparently Tom looked at Jessica like she was being overly dramatic and she didn't like that.

"And if you ever lay a hand on her again..."

"What?" Tom cut her off. "I never hurt her so I suggest you mind your own damned business."

"Take it easy," Calvin chimed in, defending Jessica.

I figured that I had better make an appearance before this got any uglier.

"I'll come home," I said as I reached the bottom of the stairs.

"You don't have to leave," Jessica said.

"It's fine, really. Thanks for everything guys." I looked at Calvin and Jessica and then walked out the door towards the car. As we drove away Tom looked at me and said, "I know you were hurt by what happened with Taylor, but don't you ever run out on me like that again. That being said, I made a mistake and I'll make it up to you, I promise."

I didn't say anything. I had a hard time believing anything he said and I just wanted to get home and have a bath by myself. I kept my distance from Tom most of that day as I did some school work and laundry. Later that evening, Tom offered to order in so I wouldn't have to cook. While eating, Tom asked, "So what's it going to take to move past this?"

I shrugged. "I don't know," I replied softly.

"I get it. I messed up, but I still love you and want our marriage to work. Don't you?"

"I do, but you've changed. I want the loving and caring man I married, not a liar and a cheater."

"I know and I'm sorry. All I can do is prove myself to you moving forward," he responded.

"No more lies," I said firmly. Then I headed to bed. Tom came in a little while later, kissed the top of my head and said goodnight.

The next few days were a little better as I took off a couple of more days from work so things could settle down. When I called into work, I asked how Rob was doing and they told me he had finally been discharged and was recuperating at home. I was relieved to hear that but I still hadn't had a chance to talk to him and find out what had actually happened. Any further questions would have to wait until I returned to work.

Friday evening Tom and I had a movie night and even shared a few laughs. One thing Tom was good at, even when I was mad at him, was making me laugh. Being close to him physically felt a little awkward because I still had images in my head of him with Taylor but he was my husband and I wanted affection as well. While watching the movie I moved closer to him and put my head on his shoulder. I think he was a little surprised, but welcomed my closeness and wrapped the blanket over my shoulder. He looked down at me and then I looked up at him. I hesitated for a second, but then reached up and kissed him. We continued kissing and one thing led to another and we ended up having sex right there on our couch with the fire in the fireplace and the movie still on.

Tom was gentle and took his time. I felt connected to him again, but admittedly I kept having images of him and Taylor that I had to keep pushing out of my mind. I didn't say anything as I didn't want to ruin the moment. I went for a shower and cried as I stood there. It had felt good to be close again, but I didn't know whether the pain of him cheating and thoughts of him being with her would ever go away. I hoped they would in time and we could move forward together. Furthermore his anger and aggression lately was still of concern to me.

The next day we went grocery shopping together and talked about summer holiday plans, including possibly going camping. I was still trying to move past all that had happened recently and work on our relationship, and Tom seemed to want to do the same.

That night after supper, while I was cleaning up, my phone rang. It was a call I had never thought I would receive.

"Hello."

"Is this Kerry?" a voice asked.

"Yes. Who's this?"

"It's Rachel," she replied.

"Oh hey!" I responded, somewhat surprised to hear from her, "How are…" then she cut me off.

"You need to listen to me very carefully. Are you alone?"

"No, Tom's upstairs."

"You aren't safe Kerry. He killed Paul!" she announced.

"Who?" I asked in surprise.

"Tom!" she responded with a raised voice.

"What!" I gasped and dropped a glass I was drying. It shattered on the floor. "What are you talking about?" I demanded.

Hearing the shattered glass, Tom shouted from our bedroom, "Are you okay?"

I managed to get the words out even though I was shaking, "I'm fine." Rachel had paused but continued,

"The night before you guys left, Tom came to our room and when Paul opened the door, Tom forced him out of the room. He had a knife and told me that if I screamed he would kill me so I didn't move.

"Once they left I followed them. They walked to the beach and I could see them in the distance in the water and there was a lot of splashing. I got nearer and could only see Tom and it looked like he was holding Paul under the water. I yelled for Tom to stop as I ran toward them, but he didn't. By the time I got to where they were, the splashing had stopped and I could see Paul face down in the water, not moving.

"I screamed and Tom came charging out of the water at me and I ran. He caught up to me and tripped me, then I remember kicking him in the face and he fell backwards. I got up and tried running away but he dragged me into the water and started trying to drown me. I bit down on his arm so he would let go of me, which worked for a split second and then he grabbed a big rock and slammed it into my head. He knocked me out cold.

"He must have thought I was dead and left. I was found by some locals who had come along a bit later and who took me to the local hospital. I was in a coma for over three weeks. When I finally woke up, I was able to recall all the events leading up to me being knocked out."

I was in complete disbelief at what I was hearing! "Tom killed someone?" I thought to myself. That explained why he had been gone so long and his bloody nose. Rachel said she hadn't been able to find the paper I gave her with my email address and it took her a while to track me down. She had managed to get my surname from the front desk at the hotel. She had still spent a couple of weeks trying to locate me, while also recovering from the incident.

"You need to get out, Kerry, it's not safe. He killed Paul," she cried.

"What should I do?" I asked her. "If I just leave, he'll suspect something's up."

"Wait until he's asleep, then leave and find a safe place. Call me and let me know you're okay."

"I will," I softly replied. Completely frightened with my heart beating out of my chest, I knew what I had to do. I was in complete shock, but I had to get out. The problem was that he would hear if I left out the back or front door because they both chimed when they were opened. The only alternative was to go through the bathroom window, but it wasn't easy to open so I would likely have to break it without making too much noise. After he'd fallen asleep I'd go to the bathroom and crawl out the window. I had no choice. I had to make a run for it.

13

The Chase Continues
(I'm Trapped!)

My eyes suddenly popped open and I gulped in a large gasp of air. Looking around, I tried to grasp where I was and I quickly remembered having been shoved into a car trunk. I started to panic: panic I would run out of air, panic that he was taking me somewhere to kill me. I tried kicking and punching the trunk lid to see if it would burst open but it stayed firmly latched. I couldn't believe this was happening. "Where was he taking me?" I wondered.

I heard a car horn and wondered whether it was the police, but they wouldn't honk, would they? Perhaps it was Jessica. She was probably driving the car I had heard drive up just as Tom had peeled away from the diner. I tried to feel around for something, anything, that could help me get out, maybe some kind of tool I could use to pry the trunk lid open or even get through to the back seat somehow. There was nothing.

All I could hear was music inside the car and occasional honking. As I felt around and tried to maneuver my body, I felt something dig into my hip. I had forgotten that I'd put the Swiss Army knife in my pocket at the diner. I managed to dig it out and to my delight it had a little flashlight on it. For such a little light it was surprisingly bright and allowed me to see my surroundings. I didn't see anything in there to use as a pry bar but I could use the knife to cut through the back seat and try to get out that way. I knew it would be risky as he would be able to see me as soon as I broke through but I really had no other choice. I started cutting through the foam and fabric so I could see the driver. I finally managed to make a small hole and could see the back of his head. If I were able to make the hole big enough to crawl through, he would definitely see me, but he was driving so he probably wouldn't be able to do much unless he pulled over, which I thought was unlikely since Jessica, or someone, was tailing him.

I started making the hole bigger when I heard shouting. Jessica was driving near him, screaming at him to pull over. He was yelling back at her with obscenities. Then I felt the car slam into what I could only imagine was Jessica's vehicle and I was tossed around in the trunk, but we were still moving. A few seconds went by and again I felt our car crashing into another vehicle. I wasn't sure if the other car had stopped or rolled into the ditch, but the sound the engine had made when it was near faded away. If it had been Jessica, I said a silent prayer that she was okay. I knew I had to try and get out as soon as possible so I went back to enlarging the hole in the seat. Finally I was able to get my whole hand through and I saw a duffle bag on the seat, more or less right in front of me so I pulled it back toward the hole to block it to give me more time to enlarge the hole before he saw me.

A couple of minutes went by as I continued cutting foam and material, slowly enlarging the hole, when I heard that same engine sound revving near our vehicle. All of sudden, I heard a screech and my body flew forward, followed by a crashing sound as the car behind us hit us. The driver of the car I was in had slammed his brakes, hoping the car behind us would hit us. We were not moving and I could smell gasoline. I wondered whether the impact had busted open the gas tank. "This can't be good, I thought.

I was shaken from the impact, but I suddenly noticed light coming through the tail-light. It must have been busted out from the impact. I tried putting my hand through the small opening to signal at the car behind us and then, as I looked through the opening, I could see Jessica in the vehicle about fifteen to twenty feet behind us. She must have hit her head on impact because she had blood on her forehead. She looked toward our car and I heard her scream my name. I kept looking through the hole, terrified of what was happening. As I tried to reposition myself, I noticed that the trunk lid was also damaged to the point that there was a light coming through where it opens. I tried pushing it open but it was jammed. I looked through the hole I had made in the seat and the driver looked like he had been rattled by the impact because he wasn't moving. I moved back to the tail-light and noticed Jessica getting out of her car and walking towards me. "Jessica!" I screamed.

"I'm coming!" she yelled back. I put my hand out through the broken tail-light and she grabbed it.

"Please help me," I cried.

"I will," she responded and tried prying the trunk open, but it wouldn't budge.

"I can't get it open," she cried.

"Please don't leave me here," I pleaded in complete fear and panic.

"I won't. I'll look for the handle for my car jack or something to pry it open and be right back."

I looked through the broken tail-light and saw her running back towards her car. As I turned my body to look through the hole in the seat, my stomach knotted. The driver was not in the front seat anymore. I quickly turned my body so that I was looking outside through the tail-light again and saw him walking toward Jessica's car. I screamed for her as she was leaned in the trunk, looking for something to pry the door open. Suddenly he was right there behind her. As she came out of the car and straightened up, he grabbed her and slammed her against the car.

She tried to take a swing at him with the car jack bar she was going to use to free me, but he blocked her and grabbed it from her, then swung at her, knocking her to the ground. I was shaking in fear. Had he killed her? I was so afraid, but I knew, now more than before, that either I escape from that trunk now or I might not have any more chances. I moved so that I was on my back and made sure that my legs were as free as possible given the cramped space I was in. Then I let loose with my feet, kicking the trunk lid as hard as I could. I kicked it repeatedly, and on the fifth try, it popped open. I climbed out, hoping that he hadn't noticed me, quickly scoped the environment, and spotted a small cluster of trees and a theme park about two hundred feet away. I had no idea whether the theme park would be open or not but it was my only option to find somewhere to hide. I took off running. Although I could still feel the throbbing from the cuts on my feet and my leg, I had so much adrenaline in my system that I barely felt what should have been a lot of pain. I looked over my shoulder. Oh my god, he had seen me and was running after me. I sent up a silent prayer. Please God, help me.

14

The Chase (The Park)

could see the trees and park getting nearer and thought that if I could hide somewhere in there, he wouldn't be able to find me and I could finally be safe. The sun was partially obscured behind some clouds and I could see the theme park lit up. The sky was getting darker as the storm from earlier seemed to be trying to start again and it began raining lightly. I reached the edge of the trees but there was a fence separating them from the theme park. I could have run to the main gate but I didn't have my purse with me so they probably wouldn't let me in for free. He would catch me for sure then. The fence was high though and I wasn't sure that I would be able to scale it. Then I suddenly thought of a plan.

I ran around the fence to the front gate, told them I had lost my shoes on a ride, was running, and fell. This would explain why my face and leg were covered in blood, and hopefully they would buy it and let me in. I asked the guard at the gate where the lost and found was. The girl at the ticket desk offered to take me to the first aid center first. I didn't want someone escorting me because that could leave me being stuck in one place and I didn't want that, not with him looking for me. I told her that I was certain I could get there on my own so she pointed me in the direction of the first aid center. As I got close, I glanced around, looking for a better place to hide. He knew that I was bleeding and that would be the first place he would look for me.

The park was massive and so many people were coming in, it must have just opened. There were rides and tent areas I could go in to hide, but if he found me in a closed space, I would have nowhere to run. I looked behind me and noticed a large Ferris wheel. I managed to sneak on while a couple was boarding. This ride would take a while to go around and buy me some time and I would also be able to see him and whether there were any escape routes.

The couple kind of looked at me oddly, probably because I looked beat-up and I wasn't wearing shoes. They asked if I was okay to which I just gave a slight nod and said quietly, "I'm fine, thank you". As the Ferris wheel started moving, I felt a bit of relief because for the moment, even if it was short, I didn't have to watch over my shoulder. As I briefly shut my eyes, I could feel the light rain hit my forehead and fresh air on my face as we started to ascend to the top of the wheel. Suddenly reality hit me and I felt anxiety building in me again. I tried looking over the edge of the bowl we were sitting in to see if I could see him.

I didn't want to expose my head too much in case he looked up and saw me. If that happened, I would be screwed for sure because all he would have to do in that case was wait for me to disembark at the bottom. I looked around and picked him out about 50 feet away. I recognized the hat and jacket he was wearing. His head was swiveling left and right, looking in all directions for me. As I came around the peak of the Ferris wheel and started descending, I kept watching, then at one point it looked like his head was facing my direction and I ducked down into the seat below the edge. I looked up at the couple and asked them fearfully,

"Can you look towards the donut stand and tell me if you see a guy wearing a cap and a blue jacket? Please don't make it obvious."

The lady made it look like she was viewing the scenery and then, still looking into the distance, very quietly said to me, "I see him. He's looking up at us." I was paralyzed at that moment with fear, thinking he had seen me and was waiting for me at the bottom.

"Wait a moment. Oh, now he's walking towards the bumper cars," she said in an encouraging voice, "You can sit up now."

Slowly I sat up and looked just over the edge. I could see the back of his head getting farther away.

"Are you sure you're okay, miss?" the husband asked me.

"I just need to get off this ride and see whether my friend is okay," I replied.

"Thank you," I said to them as our bowl came to a jerky stop to let us off. I quickly scanned the area around the Ferris wheel before getting off and started walking very quickly in the opposite direction of the bumper cars. The rain started picking up and there were even a couple of claps of thunder. There was a scary funhouse the other direction with dark halls, scary figures and secret doors. I figured this would be the last place he would look for me so I headed that way. Normally I wouldn't go into such a place as I was generally afraid of them, but considering the circumstances, it seemed the lesser of two evils. As I approached the entrance, the guy asked for my ticket. I had to think fast so I told him my little brother was in there and should have been out by now.

"I'll run in quick and find him and come right back out," I assured him.

"Make it quick," the teen-aged attendant replied, as if he were in charge of the entire park, instead of one minor attraction.

I walked in and my heart started racing. Maybe I was a little more scared than I had thought I would be. I began going through the funhouse, anticipating jump scare after jump scare. With all the events of the day, I was starting to second-guess my decision to come in here as it wasn't doing anything to calm my nerves. I continued moving through the house and came to the hall of mirrors that had mirrors that gave every angle you could imagine. There were also secret doors to enter but I wasn't really up for opening a door without knowing what was on the other side.

About ten minutes or more had passed since I walked into the funhouse and as I turned to my right my heart fell into my stomach. In one of the mirrors, there he was, desperately looking for me. My heart started racing and I kept moving my head left and right wondering where his exact location was and how close he was to me. I felt paralyzed in the moment. Just as I went to take a step forward, a clap of thunder shook the building and someone grabbed me from behind, holding me in a bear hug and pulling me through one of the secret doors. Just as I let out the start of a scream, he covered my mouth and turned me around to face him; it was Calvin. I was shaking, but couldn't have been happier to see him. Holding his finger over his closed mouth, he whispered, "He's outside the door."

"How did you know I was here?" I whispered, still shaking.

"I got a call from the ambulance. A driver came upon Jess's vehicle by the side of the highway and found her passed out. He called the ambulance. They said they were assessing her and that she had given them my number when she regained consciousness shortly after they arrived. I rushed to the scene to see her, but as I got there the ambulance had already left with Jess to the hospital. Jess texted me and told me she was okay, but to look for you. I saw some blood headed towards the ditch and the theme park was in the distance in that direction so I drove here as fast as I could. I was frantically walking around and saw you come in here. We have to get you out of here."

"So she's okay?" I said relieved.

"Yes, but she has a bad cut on her head," Calvin replied, "I need to get you to the hospital too."

"Okay, but how are we supposed to get out of here?" I asked.

"I'll go out there and see if he's still there and then you follow me. If something should happen to me, my car is parked on the east side of the park on the other side of the fence. Go to the hospital and see Jessica and get checked out."

"Okay. Thank you for coming for me," I said with tears as I gave him a hug.

"Ready?" he asked.

I nodded.

15

The Chase (The Hospital)

Calvin slowly opened the door and stepped out. He had just started turning towards me to tell me to come out when he was suddenly grabbed and slammed violently into a mirror. The glass shattered as he fell to the ground. I screamed and grabbed the doorknob to pull it shut. On the other side of the door, someone was trying to pull it open. Pulling on the knob with all my strength, I knew I couldn't hold it much longer as he was too strong. I started sobbing as I could feel my hands slipping. With a forceful pull, the door swung open. He had found me.

"Please don't hurt me," I begged.

"Why are you making this so hard?" he asked.

He moved towards me and tried to grab my arms. I started flailing wildly in all directions to prevent him from getting hold of me. I managed to hit him in the face once, but that just enraged him further and he grabbed hold of my arms and pushed me roughly against the wall, hitting the back of my head.

"We're going to walk out of here nice and calm," he explained firmly.

I shook my head and cried. I knew if I let him take me out of here, there was no telling what would happen to me.

Out of the corner of my eye I saw Calvin finally get back up to his feet. He had a large shard of glass in his hand, which he used to strike the man in the upper back. In reaction to the blow, I flinched and screamed at the same time. The man released me from his grip and fell to the ground. Calvin grabbed my hand and hollered, "Let's go!" I stepped over the man and looked down at the piece of glass sticking out of his shoulder. I wasn't sure that it would have been enough to kill him but I wasn't about to stick around and find out. Calvin yanked me along with him and we headed for the exit. As we got outside, I could feel rain pelting down much heavier that when I had gone into the funhouse. It was falling so fast and heavy, it was almost difficult to see. Calvin looked around to get his bearings and then we headed towards the edge of the theme park where he had left his car. There were fewer people around than before, which I attributed to the pouring rain but as Calvin pulled me behind him, we still had to dodge people every which way. "We're almost there!" he yelled frantically.

I took a quick glance behind us to see if the man was following us. Through the pouring rain, I could see him. I screamed, "He's coming!" We reached the fence, the same one I decided not to climb over earlier because it was too high. Calvin cupped his hands so I could put my foot in them and get a boost over the fence. I tried to push off his hands the first time, but I still couldn't reach the top of the fence and fell back down beside him. I looked back towards the man who was getting closer.

"You can do it," Calvin encouraged me.

I put my foot back into his hands and he boosted me up and I grabbed the top of the fence and pulled one leg over. My pant leg got caught and Calvin climbed up and released me from the top ridge.

"Calvin," I screamed and pointed. The man was getting very close.

"My car is right over there. Run, get inside, and start it," he ordered.

"What about you?" I cried.

"I'm coming. Go!" he replied.

I took off towards the car which was only about 30 feet away. I fumbled with the key fob but finally unlocked the door, got into the driver's seat, started the ignition and slid over to the passenger's side. The headlights came on and the wipers began moving back and forth. I could see Calvin reach the top of the fence, but suddenly the man was there and grabbed onto Calvin's leg. As he tried yanking Calvin down, Calvin managed to kick him in the face, freed his leg, and jumped down on our side of the fence. He came running toward the car and got in the driver's seat. We sat there for a second or two, looking towards the fence to see if the man was getting up. He got up, stood at the fence and stared toward us without moving. Calvin put the car in reverse, then slid it into gear and we drove away.

"We have to get you to a hospital. You don't look good at all, Kerry."

"I don't feel well either, I replied.

I suddenly felt my body go limp and I felt like I was about to pass out. My eyes closed but I could still hear Calvin's voice.

"Kerry! Kerry! Stay awake!"

I didn't respond. I must have blacked out.

All of a sudden I heard screeching tires and my body jolted forward from the sudden stop. My eyes could barely open and my body felt so heavy. I could hear sounds, but wasn't fully aware of what was happening. The trauma was finally catching up to me.

"We're here!"

It sounded like Calvin.

"Help, she needs help!"

Seconds later, I heard another voice and a car door opening.

"What happened?" asked the second voice.

"She was attacked. She may have also been drugged. She's been bleeding for a while too."

"Do you know who did this to you?" a third voice asked me.

I tried to respond but couldn't manage any words.

"Is my fiancée here? Her name is Jessica." Calvin asked.

"Go to admissions and they can help you. We'll take this one from here."

"Okay, but please don't let anyone else near her until I come back, you hear? He may try coming for her again."

I tried to beg Calvin not to leave me, but I was only able to mumble incoherently and then passed out again.

Some time must have passed. My eyes slowly opened and I could hear a slow beeping sound. My feet felt warm and they didn't hurt as much as they had. I was still a bit groggy but I could feel something over my mouth. It must have been an oxygen mask. I looked around the room:

apparently I was in the hospital. Looking down, I noticed I had an I.V. needle in my hand, probably something to rehydrate me or help with discomfort and pain. I tried to remember how I had gotten here. I had flashes of memories: the train, the diner, the car trunk, Jessica, Calvin finding me at the theme park, Calvin stabbing that guy, climbing the fence, and finally finding safety in his car as we made our getaway. But where was Calvin now? They must have dimmed the lights to help me sleep or perhaps I had a concussion. All I could think about was where was Calvin? Where was Jessica? Was he still trying to find me?

Moments later, a nurse came into the room and started talking to me, asking how I felt and whether I knew where I was. I nodded, but felt too drained to say anything. She checked me over to see if everything looked okay. While she was checking my I.V. stand, Calvin walked in. I was so relieved to see him and opened my eyes a bit more. He reached for my hand, gave it a squeeze, and told me that Jessica was doing fine. She had a mild concussion and a small cut on her head but he would be taking her home tonight. I couldn't speak but I tried to show my relief she was okay.

I heard him ask the nurse, "How is she doing?"

"She's doing okay, but she sure went through a lot. She has a large wound on her leg where she lost a fair bit of blood, but we stitched it up and it should heal in time.

Her feet were quite cut up so we cleaned out the gravel, and dressed and bandaged them. The scans indicated signs of a concussion and judging by the marks on her face and bump on the back of her head, it is likely, but we are waiting for the doctor to have a look at them. She's a very lucky woman that you found her and brought her in when you did."

"Thank you," Calvin said to the nurse as she walked away. He looked at me,

"Did you hear that, you're going to be okay." He squeezed my hand and told me he was going to check on Jessica and grab a coffee, then come back a little later. I squeezed his hand and shook my head because I didn't want to be left alone. My eyes must have shown him how anxious and afraid I was.

"It's going to be fine. I'm just on the next floor and I'll come back in a bit to see you again," Calvin reassured me. I nodded and he walked to the door, turned slightly, and waved to me as he left.

I lay there, watching nurses and doctors go by outside my room and I started to feel pain. The medication must have been wearing off. My leg and feet were throbbing and felt like they had a pulse. I had a pounding headache. I doubted whether I could get any more painkillers as I still felt a bit groggy. The nurse had just been here so she wouldn't be back for a while. I tried to shift my body so that my pillow would go under my back for better support and when I looked up and out the door, there he was, at the admission desk. The same jacket, the same cap. I could even see a blood smear near his shoulder as he stood with his back to me. He was either here for his own injuries or he was looking for me.

My eyes went big and my heart started to race. I didn't know whether I should try to scream for help or stay quiet. I stayed quiet. I saw him look around. He was definitely looking for me. I continued to watch to see what he was going to do, then he turned around and looked toward my room: he had seen me. He started walking towards my room and I knew that I had to use every ounce of energy I had to take the mask off and scream for help. My heart raced faster as he got closer. He opened the glass door and closed it behind him, then pulled the curtains across the same area so the view from the hall was obstructed. I had managed to slide the mask off enough to scream, but almost no sound came out.

"Help!" I rasped. I doubted anyone had heard me.

He walked over to my bed and placed one hand over my mouth to prevent me from trying to scream again, leaned down and whispered in my ear, "You actually thought you could run from me." He had an unnerving smirk on his face. Still covering my mouth with his hand, he looked at my I.V. stand and started fiddling with it. My guess was that he was trying to over-sedate me, or worse. I shook my head, trying to get his hand off my mouth but he was using pressure and holding me down too tightly. I started feeling the effects of the medication as he put the mask back on my face. Seconds later, the curtains were forcefully pushed back and a nurse demanded,

"What's going on here? Why are these curtains closed?"

I looked at her panic-stricken to ask for help with my eyes before I passed out again.

"Nothing," he responded, "I just figured she would like some privacy," he added.

"Well, we prefer them to remain open so we can keep an eye on patients," the nurse replied sternly.

"Not a problem," he said cooperatively.

"Visiting hours are almost over. I'm going to do some rounds and I'll be back in about 20 minutes, then you'll have to leave," she explained. The nurse took one last look at me and asked, "Do you need anything sweetheart?" I was definitely feeling the medication and tried my best to look alert and give some sign that I needed help, but I couldn't make any movements as my eyes were almost shut. Last thing I heard was him saying "Don't worry, I'll take care of her," then I drifted off.

16

I'm Not Dreaming!

could hear birds chirping and a woodpecker outside as I lay there with my eyes shut. Normally I didn't like the sounds of animals waking me up, but ever since we moved to the country I have grown to enjoy the sound of nature in the morning. I felt a spot of warmth on my back as the morning sun poked through the small gap between the curtains. My head felt a little heavy, like I had been in a deep sleep and hadn't been woken in days. I could tell this was my bed though as the sheets smelled like home. I slightly opened my eyes to confirm, saw the sun coming in my bedroom window and closed them again as I was still tired.

I thought to myself, "What kind of crazy dream was that I just had. It had all felt so real." I've had dreams that felt real before, but this one beat them all. There had been so many details and it was quite scary to think that someone I was so close to could do something like that, not only to me, but to so many others as well.

Feeling the warm sun and still a bit tired, I didn't want to get out of bed just yet. I moved my legs to feel them slide between the sheets while I remained laying on my front. I could feel some pain and tightness in my thigh and the throbbing on the soles of my feet was faint but still noticeable.

I slowly opened my eyes again, only this time I tried to look around a bit more but without moving, and I could feel something burning on my wrist. I looked up as my arm was above my head and my right hand was slightly under the pillow. A rope was tied around my wrist and the other end around the bedpost. My heart started racing. What the hell was going on?

I looked at the nightstand and saw something I didn't want to believe –a picture of Tom and me, but this picture had details that confirmed my worst fears. It was us on our honeymoon, and I had the butterfly tattoo on my foot and he was wearing the bracelet I had given him as a wedding gift. I slowly turned my head to the other side of the bed and there he was, lying beside me on his stomach, asleep, and his ball cap was on the chair next to the bed. I even tried to lift my head to peek at his left shoulder to see whether there were any signs of trauma; sure enough, there was a large bandage covering what I can only assume was the stab wound he suffered from earlier. I gasped and my eyes started tearing.

Help me! I wasn't dreaming.

To order more copies of this book, find books by other Canadian
authors, or make inquiries about publishing your own book, contact
PageMaster at:

PageMaster Publication Services Inc.
11340-120 Street, Edmonton, AB T5G 0W5
books@pagemaster.ca
780-425-9303

catalogue and e-commerce store
PageMasterPublishing.ca/Shop

about the author

Justin Weiher grew up in Fort Saskatchewan, Alberta and actively participated in all types of sports. He has always had a passion for helping others, evidenced through various career roles.

He served as a personal trainer for several years after graduating with a Bachelor of Physical Education. Justin earned a second degree, a Bachelor of Education and enjoyed teaching various grade levels for several years. His passion for learning did not stop there, as he continued on to earn a post-graduate degree in Counselling Psychology in 2016. His thesis is available in book form on Amazon as "Love That Lasts: A Guide To Healthy Relationships."

Justin's passion for traveling, movies, and the field of psychology inspired "Am I Dreaming?" His hope is that one day it will be made into a movie.

His pride and joy is his daughter. He enjoys spending quality time with his family, traveling with them to various parts of the world such as Las Vegas, Hawaii, Dominican, and Mexico.

He plans to obtain his professional designation as a psychologist and continue his journey of helping others live full and healthy lives.

www.ingramcontent.com/pod-product-compliance
Lightning Source LLC
Chambersburg PA
CBHW061133200626
46817CB00016B/1328